Kristian's War

To John:
I hope this book stirs

PETER WISAN

your sense of adventure.

13 Nov, 2017

ISBN: 1548504971
ISBN-13: 978-1548504977

DEDICATION

To my parents, Edward and Christine Wisan, who cracked
the code on education—they instilled a love for reading
and stuffed our home with books.

And

To the
"…millions who, humble and nameless,
The straight, hard pathway plod…"

PETER WISAN

CONTENTS

PETER WISAN

ACKNOWLEDGMENTS

My amazing beta readers: from story flow to character relatability, you each brought something unique and valuable to the story. My eternal thanks to: Andrew Malkasian, Deborah Duncalf, Decemae Yangkin, Dorothy Ross, Elly Loughlin, Guy Ashley, Nicolette Stephens, Renée Hardimon, Renée Reynolds, Shana Hare, Sherry Zook, and Wil Scott of Great Scott Editing.

Michael Scherer for your insightful comments and David Scherer for your energy and support.

My brothers, Captain Nathaniel Wisan (USMC) for your support and help, and Matthew, for your wisdom and final touches. Jonny Wisan, for your inspiration. Ben, for your leadership, and Jamie, for your unwavering positivity and support.

Ruth Fowler, for your encouragement and aide in crafting a better story.

My confidant, Tyler Murray, who encouraged me to refuse mediocre writing from myself.

And the true King.

PETER WISAN

GLOSSARY OF TERMS AND EQUIPMENT

AK-47 – Due to its easy manufacturing and near indestructability, this automatic rifle has been used by countless threat forces.

AO – Area of Operations. A sector of the map that belongs to a specific unit.

AR-15 - Commonly confused with automatic, military variants, the AR-15 is a versatile weapons system, typically chambered to accept 5.56x45 millimeter ammunition. Sometimes simply designated as the "AR".

9mm Luger/NATO/Para/Parabellum - 9x19 millimeter round originally developed for pistols. Generally accepted as the most common pistol round for civilian, law enforcement, and military applications.

Assault Pack - Tactical bag with enough supplies for short missions.

BC - Battalion Commander, an officer with authority over several hundred to greater than a thousand men.

Bivouac - A (usually) hasty site for encampment.

Camelbak - A hands-free hydration system.

Chem Sticks/Lights - Disposable light sources that glow in various colors. One version produces infrared (IR) light.

CO - Commanding Officer.

COC - Combat Operations Center, the central information hub for communication in the battle space.

Det - Detachment, a sub-unit, usually geographically separated from the parent command.

Engineer Tape - Rolls of white cloth strips used to mark off hazardous or otherwise noteworthy areas.

Fire Team - The squad's sub-unit; generally with four members.

Guidon – A ceremonial staff bearing a unit's emblem.

HK416 – A rifle by Heckler and Koch. The notable difference between the HK416 and the AR-15 platform is that the HK uses a short-stroke piston system.

HVT - High-Value Target.

Intel - Intelligence/information.

Klicks - Kilometers.

Lifed Out – To receive the most scalding verbal criticism of one's life.

Mikes - Minutes.

Motor Pool – An area for the storage and maintenance of tactical vehicles.

MSR - Main Supply Route.

NCO - Non-commissioned officer: corporals and sergeants.

Nimravus - A tactical knife made by Benchmade. Though not typically issued, Benchmade knives are used by many military personnel.

NVG - Night vision goggles.

Para - Parabellum, a fragment borrowed from the Latin

phrase, 'Si vis pacem, para bellum.' Translated, 'If you want peace, prepare for war.'

PFC - Private First Class.

Plate Carrier - A kevlar jacket with ballistic protection inserts. Often referred to as "flak jacket" or simply "flak".

Psy Ops - Psychological Operations.

Shemagh - A multi-purpose scarf worn primarily in desert operations.

Sig Pro 2022 - A polymer pistol developed by SIG Sauer.

SitRep - Situation Report, an update of the tactical space.

SNCO - Staff non-commissioned officer.

Squad - The platoon's sub-unit; it has 12 to 15 members. Three squads form a typical platoon.

Tango - Shorthand designator for anything belonging to the opposing forces.

T/O - Table of Operations, the ideal manpower for a given unit. Pronounced as two separate letters: "Tee-Oh".

Trijicon – A world-class optics brand with models in use by modern militaries.

Vic - Vehicle.

Whiskey - Military alphabet for the letter W, in the usage here, it is part of a predetermined code, where "Whiskey Tango" means "an enemy whose name starts with W," or simply, The Wanderer.

International Radiotelephony Spelling Alphabet (IRSA)

A	Alpha
B	Bravo
C	Charlie
D	Delta
E	Echo
F	Foxtrot
G	Golf
H	Hotel
I	India
J	Juliett (Joo-lee-ett)
K	Kilo (KEY-low)
L	Lima (LEE-ma)
M	Mike
N	November
O	Oscar
P	Papa (PAH-puh)
Q	Quebec
R	Romeo
S	Sierra
T	Tango
U	Uniform
V	Victor
W	Whiskey
X	X-ray
Y	Yankee
Z	Zulu

PROLOGUE PART 1

Kristian Anders kicked up dust as he walked down the gravel lane. His rust hair matted beneath a greasy ball cap. Carried by a river of daydreams, he tried to imagine his life after he graduated high school next week.

His wanderings brought him near a field carpeted in bright flowers. A girl knelt near the treeline. She wore a white sundress. The flowers seemed to rise in response to her beauty.

Kris stopped, unable to keep from staring.

The girl's chestnut hair was pulled into a loose braid. Her large, light eyes held mysteries. She reminded Kris of the elves in storybooks.

Something moved in the branches above her, and the motion pulled Kristian's gaze.

It was an animal. The leaves prevented positive identification, but they couldn't hide the feline sneer or the tightening muscles.

The predator's eyes fixed on the slight-figured girl.

"No!" Kris exclaimed.

Kris leapt forward and the mountain lion pounced.

His bony shoulder caught the animal in the ribs, knocking it off course. It snarled and streaked into the forest.

The girl looked up to her protector.

"You're bleeding!"

She held Kris's shaking arm and wrapped the wound with her white headband.

The adolescents sat down and re-lived the attack from each other's perspective.

They stayed in the meadow for hours, talking, listening, and losing themselves in each other's eyes until stars dominated the skyfields.

At nightfall, Kristian finally thought to ask her name. She took his hand and brought it to her cheek.

"I was wondering when you'd ask," she laughed.

"Christi."

"I'm going to call you Wildflower," he said as he realized something in his chest:

I'll never love any other woman for the rest of my life.

Long after the adrenaline from the lion faded, their hearts continued to pound.

PROLOGUE PART 2

Combat boots hammered the rocks with the sound of thunder, echoing back and forth across the tight limestone canyons.

It was thirteen years after the mountain lion.

A man sprinted through the passages, barely scraping through a rift in the rocks.

His pursuers opened fire. The bullets smashed the walls and splintered stony fragments into the air.

Evan, a muscular, blond-bearded operator, navigated through the sandy rock as quickly as possible. Forty enemies lapped at his heels, but he grinned and returned fire.

In front of Evan, another warrior sprinted. The man's black beard was full except where a long, horizontal scar ran across his jaw. Though Kasey was seventeen years senior to his thirty-five-year-old companion Evan, he still outpaced him.

The two men carried the weapons and equipment of modern warfare. Both wore coyote-colored ball caps that displayed a horizontal white cross on the front.

Ahead, daylight shone through an opening in the rock wall.

Kasey stopped to cover Evan's movement. A rocket-gunner took aim. The RPG spooled past Kasey's ear, landing far behind him. He shot the gunner.

As Evan approached the light, enemies appeared to block it.

Evan turned to another passage, but another group of soldiers moved in front of it. With all the exit points covered, the enemy platoon began to tighten.

"I'll fix them in place," Kasey said. "You complete the mission."

"Not leaving," Evan responded over his shots.

"He's the mission. You have to find him."

Taking a half-moment to weigh the words, Evan nodded affirmatively and hurled a grenade at the cluster of enemies.

Barely a beat after the explosion, Evan charged through the hanging dust.

The enemy's rate of fire quickened behind him.

Evan looked back once.

His companion crouched behind a large rock and returned fire on the closing nemeses.

Kasey winked at Evan then returned to engaging the enemy.

It was the last time Evan saw him alive.

1. STEPPING

Kris Anders stood at attention.

The sky hung heavy with a dusty shroud. The brown filter desaturated the entire land. Agro fields spread to the horizon, broken only by rustic homes toward the setting sun.

Most of Comfort County's forty thousand inhabitants stood in the city square.

Though just over thirty, Kris's clean-shaven face held eyes too mournful for his years.

A worn pink backpack pulled at his trap muscles. The black dye from the straps leeched into his chambray shirt as though he hadn't removed the shirt or the backpack in years. Under the rough nylon, the never-healing wounds broke apart Kristian's skin.

He rolled his shoulders back, relieving the pain for a moment. Perspiration lined his brow.

Like his fellow citizens, public executions usually didn't bother him.

But Kris had reason to sweat today.

*****

The night before.

BAM BAM BAM!

Kristian flailed his covers. The digital display on his tablet blinked 2:48.

He stumbled out of bed and slid into his boots. Creeping past his wife's bedroom, he tripped over her empty wheelchair. Christi's face twisted with some tormenting dream.

The pounding escalated, and Kris hurried to the door.

A middle-aged man stood on the porch. Sweat shone on his balding crown.

John Dabble? What's he doing here?

Whenever Kris stopped by the feed store, Dabble talked to him. He always had some new health craze or religion that he'd collected.

Usually, cheery and garrulous, John was now wild with fear.

He shoved a book against Kris's chest.

"I didn't mean anything by it."

Dabble looked back towards the road. Flashlight beams cut through the eerie brown haze. His pursuers were close.

"Hide it!" John directed as he ran into the night.

Within minutes, the gray-clad soldiers streamed into Kris's farmhouse.

*****

"John Dabble, you are charged with sedition and anarchy."

In the middle of the square, standing on a platform, a soldier spoke. He wore the rockers and chevrons of a Sergeant Major. His uniform was a pixelated, black-gray camouflage. His ramrod spine and perfect tan distinguished him in the sea of soldiers to his rear. A cloth nametape on his uniform read SHAME. He belonged to the Janissaires, the feared military force that controlled the region.

John stood against a wall. Chains held him. Kristian tried to avoid eye contact.

Sergeant Major Shame turned to a field-grade officer standing in the center of the formation. His uniform displayed the silver oak leaf array of a lieutenant colonel. He was the BC, Battalion Commanding Officer, of the Second Psychological Operations Battalion. Comfort County was a key region in his area of operations.

The Lieutenant Colonel's gray eyes betrayed no emotion. His ink-dark hair fell over gray skin. On the left shoulder of his uniform, like those of all his soldiers, a Velcro patch displayed a stitched dragon. Blood streamed from the hideous creature's mouth and from the victim beneath its steel claws.

"Sir?" the Sergeant Major addressed the Battalion Commander.

The officer made a pretense of deliberation before he responded simply, "Death."

*****

"Hey Kris, wait up."

The crowd streamed from the square.

The voice belonged to an old classmate, Danny Pleaser. Kris had let Danny follow him around for the first year of high school. When he heard Danny had been bad-mouthing him behind his back, their friendship had ended. That was seventeen years ago. Kris barely saw him anymore, but when he did, he felt sorry for the pitiable neighbor. Though in his thirties, Danny was still a scrawny kid just trying to fit in.

"Pretty crazy about John," Danny said.

"Yeah."

"Seems like the executions are far more frequent these days."

"Yeah."

"I thought you'd be rolling your wife around here."

"People with her condition don't have to come to these."

"Oh, right. Do you want to grab lunch some time?"

"I can't really talk, Danny, I'm sorry."

*****

Kristian crept into his backyard. Paint peeled in long strips from the decrepit farmhouse. Behind the dwelling stretched a forty-acre plot where puny corn stalks eked nutrients from the lifeless ground.

In the center of the backyard, a decaying tractor stained the soil. Kris approached the machine. Looking around cautiously, he reached under the yellow foam of its seat. He pulled out the black book.

Why did they kill John for this?

Across the front, his fingers traced gold letters announcing it as a RIFLE MANUAL.

Kristian suddenly remembered his backpack and his teeth set in pain.

"What can I do?"

The CRUNCH of boots startled him. Kristian slid the book into his pocket.

As he looked towards the sound, he noted instantly that the man was foreign, for the stranger wore a beard.

No one ever entered from the outside world. There were rumors—legend by now—that some men had broken in with good news, but that was nearly five generations ago. Kristian hadn't heard of anyone entering the district in his lifetime. Certainly no one was allowed to leave. The seventy-square mile border held all the births, deaths, and in-between years of everyone he knew.

"I'm Evan," the approaching man introduced.

He held himself with the confidence of someone with nothing to prove. Evan gripped Kristian's hand manfully.

Kristian immediately liked him.

"I serve the True King," Evan continued. "You should have seen me before I met Him. I was miserable. I thought I could solve everything with my own mind, when my mind *was* the problem."

Is he reading my thoughts?

"I was sent here to show you the way to Him. To show you the path."

Kristian noticed for the first time that Evan dressed for war.

"Life is an adventure," Evan said, as if in response to Kristian's stare.

The conversation felt dangerous.

In the weeks that followed, they met many times.

Some days they philosophized, other days they debated,

and some days they fished and barely talked at all.

And finally, Kristian dared to hope.

Maybe the King could help with everything.

One day, as they sat on the same rusty tractor where they had first met, Kristian admitted his thoughts.

"You never asked about my backpack. Why?"

"Cause that's not the most important thing. Listen, brother, whether I'm around or not, follow that path."

Evan pointed beyond the fields. On the other side of a stone wall ran a narrow country lane.

"It goes straight the whole way. Some things will try to knock you off, but if you stay on the path, you will find everything and everyone you seek."

*****

Kris burst into the house, heart pounding.

He stopped at the entrance of the living room. His wife sat with her wheelchair facing the joining of two walls. Christi's shrunken body wasted away beneath a tattered nightgown. Her brownish hair fell in an unbrushed frizz.

I want to be close to her, but she's shut me out so many times.

Kristian thought back to the week before.

*****

"Christi," he whispered.

Kris tucked a greeting card into her thin hands.

"Do you remember today? It's our thirteenth anniversary."

Christi seized the rims of her wheelchair and angled away from him.

"Say something, please," Kristian entreated.

Once every few months he would attempt a conversation, but she would always refuse to give him anything. Her large eyes, once brimming with love, now wouldn't even look at him.

I wish she would admit she hates me. Then at least I would hear her voice again.

He dropped the card on the end table. Mounded envelopes with yellowing birthdays and forgotten holidays scattered beneath it.

*****

Kristian came back to the present as he stood in the doorway.

I have to tell her. No matter what happens.

He knelt by the wheelchair.

He told her of Evan and of the King and that he was

14

considering taking a journey.

He hung on the silence.

Christi's vocal chords received from her brain a nearly-forgotten input. Her mouth twisted with great effort. After ten years without a sound, Christi finally spoke:

"Go," she whispered.

Kristian's heart leapt at the word. He took her hands.

"Christi, I'd like for you to come with me. Would you like that?"

She strained, turning to meet his gaze. Her thin lips released the gravel syllables.

"I never want to see you again."

*****

When Christi's sister, Katy Influence, found out Kristian was leaving, she arrived at the house within minutes, suitcases in hand.

She lobbed a sleeping bag at Kris then went into lecture mode. She could go for hours. How this whole path idea was insane, how he was a terrible husband, how if he had even a shred of loyalty, he wouldn't even consider abandoning his sick wife.

*****

A coffee shop stood solitary in the industrial neighborhood. Time had only partially unmade the abandoned buildings.

Inside the shop, an ancient espresso machine towered above new hardwood floors.

A sharp-eyed barista with a painfully-tight hair bun approached one of the two patrons.

"Are you gonna order something?"

Kristian lifted his slumped body from the table. The late morning sun angled into his face. His ringed eyes and stubbled chin spoke of a sleepless night.

"Just bring me whatever."

"One order of whatever," the girl pretended to write as she walked away.

I should have left hours ago.

His wife's reaction was not unexpected, but it still hurt him.

I never expected her to be supportive, but…she'll never change.

She still blames me for what happened.

Kris held his pounding head.

And the worst part is she's right.

The barista clanked a steaming mug onto the table.

"Three-eighty."

"Can you just give me some space?" Kris snapped.

"Sorry for serving you coffee in a coffee shop," the girl shot back as she returned to the counter.

Evan slid into the booth across from Kristian.

"If you're confused why life isn't perfect, don't worry."

Kris barely looked up.

"The enemy isn't worried about you when you're inactive. As soon as you become a threat, they increase the pressure. It's called pushback."

"I'm not a fighter, Evan."

What Kristian meant is that he wasn't a warrior.

"Neither was I," Evan said. "Take this."

Underneath the table, he pushed something metallic into Kristian's hand. Cold and weighty, it felt like a pistol.

"What's this?"

"You don't want to go on the path without some protection."

The bright metal derringer was the Bond Arms Snake Slayer. Its chamber accepted both pistol and shotgun rounds. The two barrels had one round each of .45 ACP hollowpoint and one shotgun .410 bore breaching round. The red capsule filled with metal powder specialized in eradicating locks.

Kristian had never touched a gun in his life.

"It's a master key. It opens any door," Evan explained.

"I don't want this!"

The barista looked up. Her eyes landed on Kristian's nervous hands. The sun glinted off the pistol's gold plating.

She slid into the supply closet, pulling a radio from her apron as she went.

"Why would I need protection?"

"Janissaires. Long ago the King's Son defeated their leader. But they still try to occupy this land. And kill any who leave it."

Evan closed Kris's fingers around the pistol.

"Put it in your belt. Do it now."

Two matte black Sport Utility Vehicles sped into the parking lot and screeched into a herringbone halt.

Evan pulled two halves of an AR-15 from his assault pack. He clicked them together with the precision and speed that come from countless repetitions.

"Everything will be explained. But you have to go. Now."

Evan jerked his head towards the back door while slamming a magazine into his weapon.

Eight soldiers poured from the black vehicles. Their shoulder patches held the dragon of the Second Psychological Operations Battalion. They braced their dark AK-47s over the car doors and settled the sights onto the coffee shop.

The wooden interior erupted into a chaos of screaming lead and shattered wood and burning phosphorous tracers.

Kristian hit the floor and low-crawled for the back door. Splinters and silverware blizzarded around his body.

He tucked the pistol into his belt, a part of him relieved to have it.

One of the attackers lifted an RG-6 grenade launcher. He fired it.

BOOM!

The back door exploded, covering the room with twisted metal and shredded wood.

Kristian changed course and wormed towards the drive-through window.

His chest rose and fell as he built the nerve to stand. Finally, he vaulted through.

Peering back inside, he saw Evan moving from cover to cover. The blond warrior returned fire.

Is Evan smiling? Kristian asked himself.

Two of the Janissaires broke off to flank the building. Kristian saw them.

They'll kill me.

Kristian ducked into an empty warehouse. He sprinted through the abandoned buildings. Snaking through the industrial complex, he worked towards the edge of town.

After a long run, he found himself next to the thin path that ran by his property, the same path that Evan had shown as the way to the King.

Kristian stepped onto the low stone wall.

A voice—or an impression—nudged him towards the path.

If I stay, they'll kill me. And they would probably torture Christi, too.

Despite the history between himself and his wife, Kristian acknowledged that he still loved her.

I can't let them hurt her. And maybe this King could restore us to what we were.

Kristian jumped from the wall. Though he had walked the country lane many times, he had never gone to the end. He suddenly noticed the rich red coloring of its soil.

As he stepped forward on the path, a dust storm swirled over the area, choking away his sight.

Two dark figures stepped from the haze.

They blocked his escape.

2. PUSHBACK

"Kris, get in here!"

Normally shrill and halting, his grandfather's voice shook the house.

It was twenty-two years before Kris stood on the path. The eleven year old hurried into the kitchen. Puh-pa pointed to the broken picture frame. A baseball-sized crack frosted the glass.

"Your grandma slaves at that hospital all day long to help sick and crazy strangers. I'm in the field breaking my back to put clothes on you, and you tear the house to shreds."

The boy couldn't help that he had the energy of a boy.

Puh-pa leaned in.

"Your parents would have wanted you to be GOOD."

He seized Kris's collar roughly.

"Never rock the boat. If you ever feel adventurous, just remember that somewhere your mother is crying when you're bad."

"Where?"

The grandfather's eyes filled with mist.

"Somewhere," he replied gruffly.

Young Kristian tried to imagine how his parents might have looked. When he thought of his dad, it was as a swashbuckler, not as someone vanilla and "good".

"Why didn't they want me?"

"Doesn't matter. If you ever want them to come back, you have to be good."

He shook Kris.

"You will be good. Promise me."

The image of Kristian's unknown mother crying was too much for the boy to bear.

"I'll be good, grandpa, I promise."

*****

Kristian faced the frightening silhouettes. The dust swirled away. Where the two men should have had camouflage, they wore flannel.

Kristian recognized them.

Danny Pleaser stood on the right. The other man had much more presence: he was Katy's cousin, Brock Offense. Kristian couldn't stand him.

"You're not going anywhere," Brock ordered.

"They want you back at the house," his small companion said.

"Christi said that?"

"No, Katy sent us out this morning," Danny explained.

"I have nothing to say to Katy Influence."

"But if we bring you back, I get to take her on a date," Danny said, becoming red.

"And it's the right thing to do," Brock added.

Kristian looked past the two men. Smooth white stones marked the path every hundred steps. It seemed that a worn cross was etched into the center of each stone, but Kristian decided it might be a trick of the light.

"If you go, you're just running from your terrible life, Offense accused. "There's nothing noble about that."

Brock's words triggered the question his grandfather used against him so many times: "Is this what your parents would have wanted?"

But now that hope had been kindled in Kristian's soul, it burned brighter than the echoes of his grandfather's words or the frowns of phantom parents.

Kristian pushed between the two men and moved down the path.

Brock pulled Danny roughly towards him and whispered something. The pair started after the searcher.

Within moments, all three men disappeared into the brown haze.

*****

Black was the common theme of the Battalion Commander's office. A dragon statuette carved from lead hunched on the steel desk.

Sergeant Major Shame strode into the large space.

"You wanted me, sir?"

The BC looked up at his senior enlisted advisor.

"Yes."

The BC gestured to his computer. A map of the county with population density overlays swirled on the monitor. Bright red pinpricks stood out in several locations.

"This machine is where I track the citizens who have become radicalized. Here's the past two years."

He clicked through the slides.

"And this is now."

The red dots multiplied by ten.

"The public executions aren't working. Our grip on the land is slipping. My superiors are threatening to relieve me."

"What if we make a special statement with the next deserter? Show the people the result of being a radical."

The Lieutenant Colonel nodded, inspired.

"His fellow citizens will take part in the event. If they don't rip him to shreds, we'll kill their families."

"The next Searcher will be a case study in pain."

The Sergeant Major's duty phone buzzed.

"Excuse me."

Shame answered. His face hardened.

"There's been an incident at a coffee shop, sir."

*****

The unimpressive town faded as Kristian moved east.

The landscape transitioned from agricultural fields to rough terrain dark with scrubby chaparral.

Kristian rounded a hill. A vast desert plain stretched away before him. Spindly white windmills dotted the landscape, their yawning arms unmoving.

Brock puffed with effort as he plodded up.

"How long before you return with us? This is pointless and you know it."

Fear showed on Danny's face as he joined the group.

"I've never been this far outside city limits."

"None of us have," Brock fact-checked. "No one has."

Without joining the conversation, Kristian again moved forward. The others soon followed.

A dust storm fed into itself on the horizon, browning out the sun.

As the trio passed under the turbine behemoths, they each considered the smallness of their lives.

Kristian didn't like his companions, especially Brock, but everyone deserved the same chance.

"I know you're both trying to bring me back, but have you thought about coming with me?"

Brock scoffed.

"Why?" Danny asked.

"Why would you stay?"

"Life is predictable. I've lived on Complacence Street my whole life."

"You'll die without experiencing a thing."

"That's a fine life," Brock argued.

"Maybe it shouldn't be."

"What if Kris is right?" Danny wondered aloud.

"Our job is to bring him back, not join in some insane quest that will end in death."

"That's true..."

"Danny, I know for a fact you don't like it in Comfort County. What if there was a life where you didn't have to worry about what other people thought?

"He's trying to manipulate you," Brock prompted.

Something rose out of the haze.

"The border."

A chain-link fence as high as four men spread in front. The dusty air hid the world beyond the fence, but the path seemed to continue on the other side.

Brock spoke first.

"You've had your little rebellion, Kris. Now we're going back. All three of us."

Kristian stepped forward without answering.

"It's electric," Brock warned. "You'll be sorry."

"You might die!" Danny said.

Kris touched a damp stick to the metal.

"No current."

He gripped the fence and tried his weight against the structure.

"If you go over that thing, you're a criminal. You can never come back."

Looking past Offense, Kris addressed Danny.

"I'd love for you to come with me, but it's your choice."

Danny's mind flashed to a recurring dream. It always started with the sound of lapping water. He would look around, surrounded by the sea. When he searched inside his little rowboat, he could never find the oars. Whenever the winds shifted, so did the course of the boat.

"I think I'll do it."

Brock's face drained of color and he began to back up.

"You're as crazy as he is," he blurted out, "I hope you two get caught."

He ran off, blustering as he went.

Kristian climbed atop the border. He balanced his pack on the crossbeam and helped Pleaser to the top of the fence. He lowered the little man down the other side.

I could still turn back.

Alone for the first time that day, Kristian reflected. A solitary being, his entire world consisted of a metal crossbeam and a cocoon of dust.

28

He realized the weight of his decision.

If I go to the other side, I'll be a criminal.

It could never be undone. His home, his friends, his family, nothing would ever be the same.

He considered the state of his life.

Why would I want them to be the same?

He jumped from the fence:

Kristian Anders, wanted man.

*****

Wind whistled through the ventilated coffee shop. Bullet holes pitted the ruined SUVs.

An anthill's worth of soldiers moved about the parking lot. One squad unrolled a spool of engineer tape to cordon off the scene. Everyone wore the same uniform as the eight deceased Janissaires. Underneath each fallen body, a black liquid pooled. It was thick and viscous, more like a foul tar than the blood of men.

The barista rubbed her arms.

Her teeth chattered as she gave an eyewitness account to one of the sergeants.

The tall Battalion Commander approached the sergeant. The soldier's body locked up.

The woman shrank behind the sergeant.

"And?" the Lieutenant Colonel questioned as he walked up.

"Sir, I've got her full interview here. There were two men. She recognized the first one, a Kris Anders."

"Really? The Anders kid is a searcher?"

"I fear so, sir. She witnessed the exchange of something. She thinks it was a weapon."

The Lieutenant Colonel's gray eyes turned flinty-black. He gripped the girl's shoulders.

"She helped them ambush our troops," the officer accused.

"Sir, there's something else. The second man matches the description of The Wanderer."

The officer stiffened. Evan, The Wanderer, was known to him.

"Get me all the security footage in the area."

The Lieutenant Colonel called to his advisor.

"Sergeant Major!"

Shame moved next to him.

Pointing a knife-hand at the terrified girl, the BC commanded her and the sergeant to stay.

He took the Sergeant Major aside.

"What man has tried to get a foothold into this county for years?"

"The Wanderer is here?"

"I can't afford to lose even a single soul, but it would be especially bad if it was the Anders kid. The Division Commanding General has mentioned him by name before. Could mean death for you and me. Or worse."

"I'll organize patrols to sweep the county."

"Do it. I want the searcher by nightfall."

"Roger that."

Sergeant Major Shame pivoted to carry out the order.

The Commanding Officer pointed back at the sergeant.

"You."

"Yes, sir?"

"Kill the waitress."

3. PURSUIT

"He's no good for you."

Katy, Christi's sister, spoke while she prepared dinner. Though thin-figured, Katy had swollen hands. She fumbled with the chef's knife. The tomatoes she chopped for a salad were nearly as red as her always-flushed cheeks.

Christi was parked in the kitchen with her.

"They always leave. That's what men do," Katy said.

Christi's expression didn't shift, but her mind fed upon Katy's words.

"Maybe I shouldn't have sent Brock and Danny. Maybe it would be better if THEY caught him."

At the word "They," Christi flinched.

"What kind of man abandons his wife," Katy continued, "for some sort of mid-life-self-serving-childish quest?"

The words echoed Christi's own emotions and began to take root in her heart.

*****

Kristian stood where he had landed on the far side of the fence. He couldn't move.

He forgot himself. The view surpassed anything he'd seen in his entire life.

A flat green country spread away to hills in the distance. Everything was brighter and more colorful than in Comfort. It seemed to be a peaceful land of cottages and babbling irrigation canals.

A signpost read, "LAND OF GENUINE EXPERIENCE".

Danny mumbled, "If only I had known..."

A sudden rumbling split the air behind the pair of men.

Kristian and Danny turned toward the sound.

Thunder.

Over their homeland, a thick gray cloud swirled endlessly. It obscured everything, from sky to ground, within the border fence. Fog, smoke, thunder, and fire commingled in a never-diminishing swirl.

The column backdropped the new country like smoke from a grease fire.

"Why didn't we ever notice it?"

"Because we were in it," Kristian answered.

Danny turned back to the green country.

"Now what?"

Kristian stepped forward on the straight path.

They began to move along it together.

"If we move quickly, I think we can get to those foothills before sundown," Kristian said.

"Where are we staying tonight?"

Kristian's mood faded as he realized they were traveling by foot through an unfamiliar land with no navigational aids and no provisions.

We don't even have a change of socks.

"We'll figure it out," Kristian said out loud.

They passed countless shuttered dwellings.

Not a soul appeared at door or window.

*****

The Battalion Commanding Officer pored over security footage in the red light of the mobile Combat Operations Center.

Inside the canvas tent, whiteboards, rainproof paper, and various sizes of maps crowded every flat surface.

A looped tape showed Evan moving and shooting.

"Where are you?" The Lieutenant Colonel wondered aloud. Hate filled his voice.

Sergeant Major Shame entered the tent.

"Sir, the last patrols are returning. They swept the entire district. So far nothing on the searcher."

"What about his wife?"

"The Battalion has had an asset on her for years. She's not a fan of her husband."

"We'll use that."

The sergeant appeared at the tent flap.

"Pardon me, gentlemen, but we've just detained someone with information."

"Send him in."

The sergeant stepped aside.

A man, silhouetted against the entrance of the tent, shrank in fear.

Brock Offense.

*****

Kristian and Danny were moving along swiftly. A two-story cottage stood beside the roadway.

A sound like a branch snapping broke their thoughts.

Around the corner of the house, a woodshed came into view.

Three military-age males stood inside it. They threw knives at a round of poplar wood.

Their leader moved across the path to block the men's route.

"I'm Spike," he said. This is Briar and Spiny."

Spike was smaller than Kris, but confident and wiry. A jagged scar split Briar's face diagonally. Muscle-bound, Spiny stood a head taller than the others.

"So?" Kristian said.

"Don't tell me you've never heard of us when we run the area."

While they were speaking, Briar angled behind the searchers. He gripped the nylon handle of Kristian's backpack and pulled sharply. Kris hit the ground hard. Spike kicked him in the ribs.

Spiny targeted Danny.

"Aren't you going to help your friend?"

He slapped Pleaser.

Danny looked at the ground. He didn't even raise his arms.

The bullying enraged Kristian. He jumped up, landing a punch that knocked Spiny unconscious.

Briar pulled his knife from the wooden target. He postured low, looking for the right moment to thrust into Kristian.

Kris reached for the gun at the small of his back. He hammered it and pointed the wide barrel at Spike's face.

"This gun wasn't made for this. But if you don't leave us right now, I will shoot your brother."

Dropping the knife, Briar helped his brother drag Spiny into the house.

Kristian and Danny wasted no time moving away from the area and towards the distant hills.

*****

Sergeant Major Shame and the Battalion Commanding Officer sat on repurposed ration boxes.

Red lamps, the only light source, streaked the interior of the Tactical Operations Center tent in sickly Christmas colors.

A staff noncommissioned officer reported in. The scars that webbed his face inspired visions of coldblooded violence. Slight scoliosis angled his shoulders up. His meticulously-shaven head enhanced the effect of his stern persona.

"Good evening, sir," the newcomer said, "Reporting as ordered."

"Staff Sergeant Past, the Sergeant Major tells me you're a master woodsman."

"Best in the Battalion, sir. I can find anyone at any time."

"Do you know what failing me means?"

"I do, sir."

"What's your take?"

"Sir, I'll have to examine the tracks and signs. For now, my best guess is he got a few hours past the fence, got scared, and bedded down for the night."

"How many do you need?"

"Just me."

Shame whispered to the BC.

"Yes," the superior officer repeated so he could see Past's reaction, "What about The Wanderer?"

A shade of worry crossed the enlisted Janissaire's face, but he instantly recaptured his stoic front.

"Do you want me to track him, too?"

"How about saying 'sir'?" the Sergeant Major growled.

"Aye, *sir,*" the Staff Sergeant repeated with an almost imperceptible level of sarcasm.

The Battalion Commander shook his head.

"The Wanderer is out of the district, could be anywhere. He'll link up with the searcher somewhere along the path. When he does, we'll get them together. How many will that take?"

"If The Wanderer is involved, two squads. More if you want them alive."

The Lieutenant Colonel nodded. He turned to Shame.

"Get the Staff Sergeant a platoon, full T/O, 40 bodies."

He turned back to the SNCO.

"Bring them back. Alive if possible."

"Easy, sir."

"We'll stake him in the town square until he dies. Let everyone see the punishment for raising your head. Understood?"

"Yes, sir."

"I want you on the road twenty mikes from now."

*****

The sun's lower curve dipped below the horizon. Long shadows conjured images of grotesque creatures. Hay bales became shapeless ogres in the twilight.

"It'll be dark soon," Danny said.

And that means only one thing, Kristian thought.

Danger.

Kristian lengthened his steps.

His past pulled on him with steel hooks. But he still dared to hope he could have a future.

Rummaging through his catalogue of regret, his thoughts turned back to her.

With everything I did to her…

"She'll never forgive me."

Danny looked up.

"Who, Christi?"

"I'm sure you've heard about us."

"I heard some rumors, but never knew what was true," Danny said. "What happened between you two?"

As Kristian weighed where to start the tale, he and his companion approached a crossroads. The way split into three.

The middle path had no signpost and continued straight up a hill. The other roads skirted around the base on both sides.

A boy leaned against the signpost.

"I'm Zakary Alternate," he said.

He was stylish, the kid who buys the latest clothes but pretends to be the one who invented the trends.

"Where are you going?" the boy asked, trying hard to appear disinterested. His cooler-than-thou attitude put

Kristian on the defensive.

"We were planning to take the middle path."

"Really? The middle path? That's surprising. But of course you couldn't have known."

Curiosity overcame Kris and Danny.

The kid paused to enjoy the knowledge he lorded over the strangers.

"Look behind me. There are three ways you could go. One goes up the mountain, two are paved and flat. But—"

He gestured behind him. The middle way cut switchbacks up the steep hill. Smoothness paved the left path, whose signpost read GOODENOUGH. Gray hedges grew along the right path. Its sign bragged the way to the twin cities of LEGALISM and RELIGION.

Zakary leaned in.

"—They all lead to the same place."

Kristian looked away.

What was it Evan said? Something about staying on the path. But he didn't say if there were any detours or turns.

The left and right branches certainly looked the same as the middle one.

Kristian half-noticed that though the red path had no signpost, the white stones still marked it and not the alternate routes.

The kid continued.

"I guarantee they're all the same."

Seizing on the travelers' silence, he gestured to Kristian's pink backpack.

"You're going to break your back with that thing. Why put yourself through the extra agony?"

Kristian remembered the throbbing pain of his upper back.

"If you're wondering why you should push up a mountain if they're all the same, you're smart. Or you can break your body for no reason."

Danny stared at the trail under him, hoping that he would go unnoticed by the sharp-tongued kid.

"What about you?" Alternate questioned him.

"I'm new to this journey," Danny deflected, "He wanted me to come along."

"And you do everything your friend tells you to do?"

"I think for myself."

"You'd love the left path. It's unchallenging. It would be a great fit."

"I don't want to go alone."

"Cause you're not your own man?"

"I am."

"So it's that you don't trust me," Zakary accused.

"Oh, I do trust you!" Danny wailed.

Kristian interjected.

"How do we know you're one of us?"

"Look," the kid said with the air of a rocket scientist explaining the concept of addition, "You've been traveling for two minutes. I live here."

The boy put his hand on Kristian, right where the backpack dug into the skin. If the pain had been dull before, it now shot through his nerves. Kristian ground his teeth to keep from screaming.

The boy whispered.

"Take my word for it. Your path doesn't get any easier."

Kristian ignored his uneasy gut. He considered the pathway on the right.

It does look inviting.

And flat.

4. ABANDONED

Christi awoke in her cold bed.

Harsh wind beat the slats of the old farmhouse together. The uncanny sound at such a late hour chilled Christi's bones.

What time is it?

In the grays of the unlit night, hushed voices arose from the next room.

Christi recognized the rise and fall of Katy's voice, but an unidentifiable masculine speaker responded.

Who is he? Probably one of Katy's many boyfriends. But most have been over here. I don't recognize his voice at all.

She had a realization that raised her skin.

Maybe he's the man who convinced Kris to leave me.

What did Kris call him? Ethan? No. Evan.

She wanted to see his face.

What kind of man convinces someone to run from everything they know? I bet he looks like a used car salesman.

She pulled her shriveled body from the bed. She slid across the floor with effort.

Using all her strength to lift her unyielding body to the keyhole, Christi peeked into the living room.

Katy faced Christi's door. A middle-aged figure paced across the room. Christi's searching eyes only caught his back.

She knew immediately he couldn't have been one of Katy's boyfriends. She was sure that he wasn't Kristian's friend Evan either.

He wore a uniform.

The Janissaire had slick, dark hair. As he strode back and forth in front of the cold, cindered fireplace, his right hand, like an old gunslinger's, never strayed far from the grip of his holstered pistol.

"You're sure she can't hear us?" the Lieutenant Colonel asked.

"She fell asleep hours ago. The bed is across her room. Trust me, she's not going anywhere."

The Battalion Commander nodded.

"Shame said you've been an agent for the Battalion for years. I have new orders for you."

"About Kris?"

"No. He's beyond your influence."

"I didn't think he'd actually leave the city."

"He left the county."

Christi clenched her ivory fingers into fists.

So he did leave.

"I want to be very clear," the BC continued, "Under no circumstances can your sister discover he got out. As you know, husband and wife combinations make some of the most powerful searchers."

He doesn't have to worry about that. I wouldn't follow Kris anywhere.

Katy laughed. "Christi is a vegetable," she reassured the officer, "She's useless."

The cruel words filleted Christi's soul.

"She does everything I tell her," Katy said.

"You've done well with her. Still, in these matters, unexpected recoveries have been observed."

The officer retrieved his overcoat from the back of the sofa.

"Where's your radio?"

"In the barn."

"Keep monitoring the net. I'll send periodic instructions."

Adjusting his cover with military snap, he walked towards the door.

"Keep your sister from the path. If she's busy hating her husband, she won't even consider it."

The Lieutenant Colonel departed into the night.

Katy watched through the window. The brake lights of the BC's tactical vehicles soon blinked into the distance.

Katy moved to extinguish the solitary lamp that lit the room.

As Christi pushed her body away from the keyhole, the aged floorboards creaked beneath her.

Katy bloodhounded the sound.

Crossing from the lamp to the door, Katy put an ear to the wood and closed her eyes. It focused her senses.

"Christi, honey, are you awake?" Katy whispered.

An old grandfather clock ticked the only response.

Christi's breath was arrested. Her one friend, her own blood, was a spy. As Christi lay crumpled by the door, she reaffirmed what her mind had waterwheeled over and over through countless sleepless nights:

You can't trust anyone. They will all hurt you.

Outside, the wind continued to gust. An old weather vane creaked in protest.

Satisfied that the noise was only the house settling, Katy moved away from the door and went into the backyard.

Christi released her thin lungs.

She choked in a marsh of misery, losing the will to claw for the surface.

Her inner narrative mocked her. It taunted her for all the times she had resisted this thought:

I am entirely alone.

*****

"Radio check, over."

Katy keyed the handset.

She sat in the loft of the old barn. Broken farm equipment lined the gray walls.

The military-issued radio set popped with spirit. A young radio operator on the far end answered.

Nearby re-transmission sites extended the signal.

When not in use, Katy would pull a heavy canvas tarpaulin over the radio and move the ladder. Not that it was necessary. Christi's weak limbs could never support her up to the loft.

But Katy Influence's primary ally was misinformation.

She couldn't risk Christi hearing an alternate narrative.

After the radio check, Katy monitored the net for a long while. Occasionally a coded message came through about the progress against Kris. Finally satisfied that she could receive and transmit without issues, Katy shut off the set.

She pivoted towards the ladder. Her body froze in temptation. Something called to her.

Her eyes moved to the corner of the loft. A blanket of dust lay over the junk that filled the barn.

Katy scanned left and right out of habit. Her mouth watered in anticipation. She peered through a window to verify that the old farmhouse slept then pulled a paper cup from her pocket.

It's late…but a drink can't hurt.

In the corner of the loft, hoarded beneath a row of cobwebbed chairs, lay a bottle of liquor: it was the only dustless object in the barn.

Maybe she drank because her addiction was too strong to oppose. Maybe she wanted to dampen the guilt of aiding her brother-in-law's pursuers.

They'll kill him.

The honey-colored liquid swished seductively, and she let her moral introspection evaporate.

"I earned a drink," she justified to the air.

The bottle empty and the sun stirring, Katy Influence

finally collapsed senseless into the dust.

*****

Three sets of footprints indented the soil below the border fence.

Staff Sergeant Past studied the ground with a red flashlight beam.

Brock stood nearby. The burly soldiers on either side dwarfed him.

"This is where they went over?" Staff Sergeant Past said.

"Yes. I invented the fact that it was electric so he'd stay," Brock said. "I tried to talk them out of it."

"You failed, didn't you?"

"Maybe he came back already."

"If he was in the district, we would have found him."

"I was only trying to help," Brock mumbled sullenly.

"Shut your whine well and let me think."

A lance corporal leaned from the driver's seat of a tactical truck.

"We mounting up, Staff Sarn't?"

Past considered for a moment.

"If we use the trucks, the searchers will hear us and

conceal themselves. Could prolong the pursuit. Here's what we do. The platoon is going to hop the fence and go on dismounted from here. Take the other drivers and go around. Re-establish contact with us as soon as you get all the trucks outside the fence line. After that, the vics will trace behind the platoon for the rest of the mission."

The soldier nodded; he ignited the engine and the ten trucks pulled away.

The Staff Sergeant tossed a roll of bills to Brock Offense.

"Get out of here."

For the second time that day, Brock melted back towards Comfort.

Past gave the hand and arm signal for "assemble". After briefing the key leaders, he motioned them forward.

The Staff Sergeant vaulted the fence.

On the trail of the searchers.

*****

Barbs of infrared light poked through the darkness. Without night vision goggles, the IR lines escaped detection by the naked eye.

The Staff Sergeant and his platoon ghosted the darkness like candles through cobwebs.

They approached the same crossroads where a conflicted Kristian had stood recently.

The Janissaires' NVGs captured no human movement.

A grenadier's ragged whisper cut the night, "I got something, Staff Sergeant."

The Staff NCO slid out from the darkness.

"What is it?"

The grenadier pointed to a solitary pink thread at the intersection.

"The searcher's burden."

The Staff Sergeant analyzed the three paths.

"Which one did they take?" one of the junior enlisted soldiers asked.

Past shone his light on the left path, then the middle, then the right. Between packed dirt and gravel, the dry roads betrayed no footprints.

At any given time, the platoon could be split into three sub-units, each numbering approximately thirteen.

Past called up the leaders.

"Break into squads. Each one traces a path. I'm with First Squad. Whichever Squad Leader finds him first, light up a red star cluster."

He tapped a flare like the one each of his sergeants carried.

"The rest of the platoon will converge on your location," he continued.

"Should we worry about his companion?" one sergeant asked.

Past spit into the black night.

"Interrogate the friend if you come across him. But the searcher is my priority."

"Alive?"

"Try to take him that way, but if it looks like he's getting away, smoke him."

*****

Danny Pleaser moved down a wide road. It skirted the left side of a mountain. Ornamental trees rose next to the highway.

His thin frame rattled. His internal dialogue questioned him relentlessly.

Why did I leave home? My life was good.

Danny wished he cared less about what people thought and more about what he wanted.

He stopped every few feet to listen for imagined foes.

For the first time, his apprehension wasn't unfounded. He heard something. It was the unmistakable sound of a cough.

He racked his brain.

Are humans the only animals that cough?

Danny slid behind a tree.

The soft rhythm of cloth on cloth met his ears.

A wedge of soldiers slid into view. They followed the road wordlessly, rifles at the ready. Pleaser knew their uniform; it was the same pattern worn by John Dabble's executioners in the town square.

Janissaires.

Danny tried to hold his breath.

They can hear me, I know it.

Contradicting courses of action flooded his mind.

I should stay hidden. Then find the main path again.

But why am I afraid? I didn't do nothin' wrong. I'll say Kris made me come then abandoned me. I got lost looking for the way back. That's basically true.

Danny stepped out.

"I'm here."

The squad coiled into a wall around him, prodding his ribs with the hard points of their rifles.

"I'm a victim! He made me go with him."

None of the soldiers heeded his choked cries.

Staff Sergeant Past broke the ring of bodies. He grabbed Danny by the throat.

"Where's the searcher?" His bellowing voice shook the timid man.

"Please, I'll tell you everything. Just don't hurt me."

"You will tell me everything. And I will hurt you."

The soldiers kicked Danny to the dirt. Their heavy boots dug into his limbs.

"Do you know how we found you?" Past taunted. "Your old friend Brock. He's back in your town doing our work now."

"I don't know what Brock told you, but Kris made me do it. I swear, I didn't want to go. Please don't kill me."

"I want the searcher's last known location. That's a reason for me not to kill you. But it doesn't mean you won't suffer."

The Staff Sergeant pulled a vial of jet-black liquid from his bag. Its label read, "REGRET". Past loaded a syringe with the thick substance and shoved it straight into Danny's heart.

Pleaser fought it at first, but once he caved, the poison worked swiftly. His mind flooded with his most terrible memories. Vivid pictures of his worst decisions, his darkest actions, swarmed his mind.

"I'll do anything! What do you want to know? Please, please!"

Past nodded. He reached as though he were going to pull the needle out, but he turned it sharply. Pain corkscrewed through the prisoner's body.

Danny Pleaser's words fell out. He even recounted how he did the whole thing so Katy would notice him.

As he approached the end of his story, Danny's voice elongated into a near-screech.

"I never wanted to leave the district! Kris made me do it then he left me at the crossroads. I got lost and when I saw you guys, I thought you could help me."

"I'll help you."

Past held REGRET in front of the man's eyes.

"That's everything, I swear!" Danny screamed.

"Where is he now?"

"Last I saw, he turned off the main path. He went to the right. That was a couple hours ago."

"Did he say where he was going?"

"Not a word. Please let me go home. I've told you everything."

"I know."

The Staff Sergeant un-holstered his pistol.

"But I'm out of reasons to keep you alive."

*****

A long cloud slid in front of the full moon, painting the

land in black.

The weak illumination of the night now hid Kristian's progress from his own eyes.

He rolled his ankle on a slick stone, and pain shot through the joint.

How long has it been since I lost the path?

Kristian admitted to himself what he had known since he left the crossroad.

I messed up.

He scanned the night, hoping to see a white marker stone.

As he tripped slowly up the trail, he felt the ground steepen beneath him.

That's a good sign, he thought. *Maybe I'll link up with the path soon.*

Hope moved his tired legs.

Suddenly, out of the darkness, an unfeeling brightness appeared. It was counterfeit light, as though a ray of sunshine had painted Kristian's arm with frost.

A robed figure stood in the center of the beam.

"My name is DISCOURAGE," the newcomer said.

Kristian found no answer.

"I was sent here by the King. These are His gifts to

you."

The bright being held two leaden objects. He made a pretense of ease, but the kettlebells were clearly mighty weights. Each had one stamped word: LAW and EFFORT.

"The King orders you to add these to your bag."

Kristian's stomach tightened again.

I know I probably shouldn't have listened to that kid at the crossroads. But this guy...who am I to question the King's messenger?

Kristian decided on a compromise.

"I'll take them if you tell me where the path is."

"Of course," the stranger leered. "That's why I am here."

The being gestured to the right of Kristian.

"You have been parallel to the path this whole time. If you go only ten steps to the right, you will find it."

Kristian reached for the kettlebells.

Something happened that made him question how he could have ever believed DISCOURAGE.

A true light shone from the darkness. It revealed the full nature of the being in front of Kristian. DISCOURAGE transformed into a small creature with waxy skin and sunken eyes. Chains connected his wrists to the kettlebells. Blood stained his lips.

He meant to feed on me.

A beautiful woman stood at the source of the new, pure light. Her height rose like a frieze of a medieval queen, stately and strong. The light in her clear voice cut the night to shreds.

"Away, you."

Without a word, the creature obeyed, fading into the night.

The woman turned to the searcher.

"I am Grace," she said. "And you are becoming Kristian."

"I lost the path," he confessed.

"But that is why I am here," she laughed.

Something in her smile triggered a memory. Kristian remembered when he broke his leg as a child. His grandmother splinted it. She made his favorite cake and whispered all afternoon that he was her favorite grandson. Grace's smile expressed that same love.

She pointed a finger, and golden light shone from it, coring the darkness like an apple. Only a few steps to Kristian's left was the path. He'd been near it the entire time.

Kristian started towards it. Grace brought her arm down.

"You must see one thing first."

She extended her left arm, illuminating the night in the other direction. A massive drop fell off below Kristian. The little creature had intended for Kristian to fall to his death. The dirt beneath Kristian's foot crumbled and fell into the blackness. He jumped back.

"Many have taken this road and fallen," Grace explained. "Don't look so sad. I am not going to punish you. But stay vigilant. Take care who you trust along this road."

"I don't deserve your kindness."

"I don't keep accounts, and I don't use words like 'deserve'," she answered.

"Then I don't know what to say."

Grace smiled maternally.

"Return to the path. That will be enough."

Kristian nodded and started on his way.

"And remember that shortcuts often take longer," she called after him.

He followed the light. Once the solid path held his feet, he felt once again that he had a future and a hope.

He jumped in joy and ran upwards, steps illuminated by the cheery glowing marker stones.

The clouds departed, and the bright lunar crescent caught his gaze.

I hope my wife sleeps in peace under the same moon.

*****

The moonlight shone through the window of the farmhouse. Christi was still piled on the hard, uneven floor, a mound of paper skin and brittle bones.

Her chest ached.

Maybe it's a heart attack.

Her mind turned to her long-distant husband.

Remember the date when Kris robbed you of everything?

On that historic day, she had decided that the heart is safe from hurt only without love. So she had brickwalled herself.

But tonight on the floor, unable to move, both due to her soul-pain and from the strain she put on her long disused muscles, with her husband lifetimes away, and her only family in the world a traitor, Christi didn't know what to do.

So she cried.

Christi, who had barricaded herself from all feelings, finally felt something. And it was as bad as she remembered.

She had worked night and day for ten years to ensure she would never be hurt again. But the very act of pushing everyone away had trimmed a neat square from her armor. Now through the gap came a single word, a word that cut her soul to the marrow:

Abandonment.

No, I'm beyond abandoned.

It was worse. There <u>were</u> people in her life. But...

In the whole wide world, there is no one you can lean on. There is no one you can trust.

Christi finally accepted it as diktat.

I'm alone.

Katy's words had wounded, but they were in character. They had served to open the floodgate of emotions against Kristian.

The man whom she had trusted most in the world, who had caused, no, who had authored all her problems, had abandoned her.

After everything he did to me, he just walked away.

"I hope they catch him," she admitted hoarsely to the unfeeling walls.

What he did is unforgivable.

Then through bitter, clenched teeth, black soul communing with the black night, she whispered in acid syllables.

"I hope they kill him."

5. REUNION

Obsidian, the night. Impersonal.

Kristian checked his steps cautiously. Several weeks had passed since his folly at the crossroads.

He made his way through endless walnut groves. He had seen no husbandmen, so he filled his pockets. Stopping to flatten the nuts between two stones, he wondered how many pounds he had lost since leaving Comfort County.

As he tasted the delicious wild edibles, he decided his weight didn't matter.

At least I'm starting to become a little more streetwise.

The clouds drew back from the moon. Kristian lifted his hands. They were stained a dark brown from the walnut husks.

Then again, maybe not.

A terrifying sound shattered the night.

The roar of a lion.

This could be no mountain lion. It sounded like a mane-covered, 400-pound beast. Kris knew them from television.

The roar vibrated through the ground, up through Kristian's soles, and into his core.

He scanned the blackness, searching for the animal, but he couldn't see anything.

Maybe if I stand still it won't see me.

Though he was tempted to run, Kristian resolved that he would never be killed from behind.

If I'm gonna die, I'm gonna meet death eye-to-eye, predator-to-predator.

The thoughts were heroic, but Kristian managed only to inch his feet forward.

Something appeared out from the darkness: the unmistakable hollow eyes of a carnivore. Strength drained from Kristian's limbs.

A renewed roar rang his ears.

Kristian expected death at any moment, but the hungry eyes did not advance.

He's toying with me. He wants me to run.

Blood returned to Kristian's limbs. He prepared to

fight for his life.

Let's go.

The unblinking eyes held on him, so Kristian stepped towards the animal. No sprint, barely a shuffle. But he moved forward in the face of certain death, and that is what counts.

Kristian gained confidence in the advance, and the predator's eyes began to retreat.

As Kristian neared the animal, something seemed entirely wrong. Expecting tangled mane and muscular haunches, what he saw shocked him.

Iron crossed into a small cage. A microphone rested between the bars. A cable ran from it to a black box to a large speaker.

An animal strode the length of the cage. A predator, but only feared by mice. The house cat (more of a kitten, really) blinked.

Kristian picked up the black box: a pitch modulator. It ratcheted the kitten's pitiful mewls into throaty roars. The word FEAR stood out on the animal's collar.

Kristian roared with laughter.

One strike with a branch busted the rusty padlock. The merciless kitten pushed out and tried to attack Kristian's leg. He nudged it away.

The animal sulked into the forest, unaccustomed to confrontation.

Kristian's boot shot into the speaker.

ZICK!

A bullet cracked the air. It struck the modulator. Bright muzzle flashes stamped the darkness.

Four enemy soldiers burst from the trees behind Kristian.

One grabbed his arm.

The searcher broke free and raced away. Automatic rifles chattered away behind him.

I only have two rounds in my pistol.

The pursuers gave chase, their lights tracking Kris as he zigzagged through the orchards.

The trees suddenly thinned, and a plunging fall appeared to Kristian's front. He couldn't stop in time.

Contorting his body through the air, he gripped the side of the cliff. To his right, the path turned into a narrow slip of stone that bridged across the chasm.

He pulled himself to safety as his enemies drew near.

Sprinting to the shale bridge, Kristian crossed as quickly as possible without losing his balance. A fall would result in certain death.

If I make it across the bridge, maybe I can lose them.

The bullets tracked Kristian's heels. The chipped rock stung his skin, and the Janissaires gained on him.

Though his body was strong from years of manual labor, Kris wasn't a runner, especially at this altitude. Each step jostled his lungs. He prayed for air.

Kristian reached the far side of the canyon. A loose stone slipped beneath him. Aching legs gave out, and his face pitched into the jagged rock.

The pursuers surrounded Kris and slammed him to the ground. Knees and elbows dug into his bones.

The washout effect from their bright lights blinded Kristian.

"Why did you run, searcher?" one of them taunted.

This will not be my end.

Kris slid his hand slowly behind him.

A second fire team appeared from the grove. They made their way towards the four captors.

Two soft but significant sounds crept out of the blackness behind Kristian:

The *shlick* of a pistol rubbing Kydex, and the sound of a blade being skinned from a nylon scabbard.

Evan.

For most of his life, whenever Kristian heard the word good, the image he conjured was a boy with parted hair, who acted the angel near grown-ups, but bullied the smaller kids when unsupervised. In this moment, Kristian's definition changed. Good meant Manliness.

Valor. A brawny, bearded operator with deadly skills that had been acquired for the defense of others.

Between Evan's pistol and blade, the four aggressors went down before comprehending the threat.

Three more soldiers closed in. Evan shot the first. Another knocked away his pistol.

Two enemies engaged Evan in hand-to-hand combat, but his years on the road showed in his fighting skills. His knife darted with unbelievable speed.

He dispatched one soldier. The other fumbled with a shotgun. Before he could pull the trigger, Evan cut him down.

"Evan!"

Kristian gestured to the last enemy, thirty paces away. The enemy sergeant rifled through a rucksack.

Evan raised his rifle and shot twice.

The sergeant teetered on the edge of the shale bridge. The notepad with the barista's interview poked from his cargo pocket.

He refused to go down. He clutched the 40-millimeter red flare. He slid it into the chamber of the under-barrel grenade launcher.

Evan knew what the signal would mean. He shot the squad leader five more times.

The body tumbled off the arch to certain death, but the soldier's last reflex compressed the trigger.

A flare launched into the night. It burst into red ripples that cut the sky like fireblood.

Evan pulled Kristian to his feet.

"We have to move, brother. He'll know where to look for us now."

"Who?"

Shots erupted on the far side of the arch.

Staff Sergeant Past charged at the head of thirty Janissaires.

Evan launched into a sprint. He looked back periodically to ensure his companion was safe.

Encouraged by Evan, Kristian now ran better. Over uneven terrain and with minimal loads, the two men soon outpaced their pursuers.

*****

Katy sat in the barn.

She monitored the radio traffic between elements. It helped to alleviate the slow pace of farmhouse living.

Staff Sergeant Past's voice crackled the set to life.

"SitRep, over."

"Go for Bravo Charlie, actual," the Lieutenant Colonel responded.

The call signs showed that the Staff NCO spoke directly to the Battalion Commander.

"Made contact with objectives."

"Mission status?"

"In progress."

"Do you have the HVT?"

"Negative. Primary target Whiskey Tango is with him."

"Do you have line of sight?"

"Not at this time."

"Get it."

"Roger. One more thing. We took casualties."

"How many?"

"Eight KIA."

Katy smiled. She hated Staff Sergeant Past. The pause meant he was about to get lifed out by the boss.

"Come see me," the officer ordered.

*****

The boy, Sage Influence, sensed Christi's pain. It hurt him. Sage's emotional intuition exceeded his fifteen years.

Sage sat in the farmhouse's living room, stealing looks at his crippled aunt.

On this rare visit that his father allowed, his mother, Katy, was already whiskey-gone.

Sage himself, his older brother, and a love for the bottle; those were the only things his parents had in common.

He remembered when Aunt Christi was young and beautiful. Sage had always admired her. He was only five when she lost her spirit. He remembered when she transformed from the fun-loving aunt into who she was today. He remembered when all the fun and youth drained from her. But he could never remember why. And no one talked about it.

How can I restore her?

The house's drafty old attic sprang into his mind. Years before, when he and his brother played besieged soldiers behind their dusty box fortress, they uncovered a crate full of memories.

The photograph.

Its beauty had made Sage cry, and his brother had mocked him for it.

Sage determined to recover the picture.

He planned to leave the image on Christi's nightstand after the household slept.

That will heal her.

His mouth scrunched up resolutely.

And maybe she'll be happy again.

*****

Evan and Kristian covered the valley quickly under the starless sky. The path cut through yellow clay hills.

Two nights had elapsed since the enemy encounter.

Kristian wished he had a rifle. He kicked himself for not grabbing one from the fallen enemies.

Evan illuminated the path with the light attached to his AR-15. Kristian walked behind, feeling insignificant in the unknown territory. With every rustle of the bushes, every night noise, he wondered if the enemies were closing in.

Evan traveled unbothered. As he walked, he kept reaching for a black book in his cargo pocket. Each time, he would read a couple lines by the moonlight, then put it back.

Kris pulled out his own copy. He hadn't touched it since John Dabble's execution.

"What's in here?"

"Instructions on how to use the rifle."

"Not much good without a weapon."

"There's more than that. The Manual teaches tactics and outlines enemy strategies. It even tells stories of great warriors who fought along this same path."

"Where can I get a rifle?"

"We'll take care of it soon enough. In the meantime, start learning the Manual."

Kristian cracked the book to the first page. The opening words belittled the dark. They described a wonderful young world where the King had commanded life from a void.

Kristian became aware of his deep yearning, one he had felt before when watching a sunset or when floating on a lake.

As he read, the night lightened. He became bolder, and the twilight sounds affected him less.

He stopped worrying about the enemy.

*****

Emotions flooded Christi's soul.

What am I doing with this?

Her parchment fingers traced the faded sepia. The frame held two crazy-love kids on courthouse steps.

In the still, young Christi's face fell back in laughter. Her fingers cradled her man's lapel.

Christi remembered the crotchety passerby who had taken the photo. The stuffy woman had displayed her evident contempt for young love.

"Yes, yes, let's get on with it," she had said.

Her hurry resulted in a photo that was blurred and slanted. But it couldn't hide the affection of the kids.

I want that again, Christi admitted to herself.

"Take your handholding somewhere <u>decent</u>," the woman had scolded.

Despite herself, Christi smiled at the memory.

Katy burst in. "I'm the best shopper in the whole world. You've never seen eggs so cheap—"

Her eyes fell on the photo. All color fell from her cheeks.

"Where did you get that?"

*****

Katy lifted the handset to her dry lips.

"Bravo Charlie, there's been a complication."

*****

Alongside the path, meadows ran. Evan and Kristian enjoyed the bright sunshine.

A solitary maple tree shaded a patch of the trail, and beneath it, a stranger napped. He was dressed like Evan, but a boonie-style hat covered his eyes.

Evan motioned for Kristian to stay then crept up mischievously. He stooped to take the stranger's rifle.

A pistol hammer clicked at the man's side.

"Don't," a voice said from under the hat.

The stranger lifted it up. On seeing the wanderer, his face broke into a smile.

"Evan. Of course it's you."

The lanky stranger stood up, head and shoulders taller than the other men.

"It's good to see you, Loak."

Evan motioned Kris to join them.

"This is Loak. They used to call men like him 'Seers'."

"Today, I wish I weren't one. I have bad news."

"Let's hear it," Evan said.

"This is a personal message."

Kristian nodded and moved up the road.

Loak pulled the sling from Evan's rifle and bound his own hands with it.

"The owner of this sling will be captured and killed."

"Not the first time I've gotten this word. Where?"

"City of Currently."

*****

The Staff Sergeant rode in the passenger seat of the tactical vehicle.

Natural meadows gave way to high clay hills. The vehicle lurched around the sharp turns. Past stared out the window, unaffected.

Around a hill, the battalion bivouac site came into view.

Soldiers buzzed over the hills, striking camp. The Lieutenant Colonel wandered the worksite with hands folded behind his back. Sergeant Major Shame followed in step behind him.

A young PFC worked to tear down the command tent. Instead of pulling at the stake, he yanked the line that held it.

The motion tore a wide rift in the tent fabric. A pocket of rainwater drained through the hole, sizzling a large radio inside.

The Lieutenant Colonel whispered an order to Shame. The Sergeant Major grabbed the soldier and directed him towards the treeline. Shame's pointer finger indented the release of his pistol.

Past observed the whole thing in horror. His truck braked to a halt. He jumped out and hailed the boss with a "Good morning, sir!"

After recounting how the two men had escaped, Past waited for the officer to boil over.

The Lieutenant Colonel stared with ice eyes. After an eternity, he spoke.

"How are you going to fix this?"

"Sir, I'm going to intercept them between here and the

next city. They won't be able to reach it by this evening. My troops should arrive—"

"Should?"

"My troops *will* arrive after the travelers have settled in for the night. We'll catch them unaware."

"Make it happen."

"Aye, sir."

The Lieutenant Colonel scanned the working soldiers for a target.

"I have to go all the way back to the searcher's wife. Once I'm done, myself and Sergeant Major Shame will meet you in the city tomorrow."

"Aye, sir."

The Staff Sergeant turned to go.

"Staff Sergeant, do you remember Lieutenant Legion?"

Past nodded.

"Yes, sir."

"That's failure to me. Get out of here."

The Staff Sergeant shook his driver awake roughly.

The vehicle sped away. After giving the junior soldier a high-volume pep talk, Past turned silent.

He didn't speak for most of the ride. The radio

operator, new to the Battalion and still unseasoned, attempted a conversation from the backseat.

"Staff Sergeant, who was Lieutenant Legion?"

*****

Coincidentally, Past and the Battalion Commanding Officer had checked into the unit on the same day. During the ceremony where the Lieutenant Colonel accepted command of the unit, a certain First Lieutenant named Legion was made the "guest of honor".

The week before, a high-profile prisoner had successfully escaped while the Lieutenant was the duty officer.

The new Battalion Commander had made an example of him.

More than a thousand soldiers attended the proceedings. They shouted with savage affirmation at the execution.

The young officer's severed head stood atop the Battalion guidon for months afterward.

The empty black eyes cautioned a passing soldier of one thing: Never fail the Lieutenant Colonel.

*****

Razor wind chiseled between the cracks in the truck.

Past shivered and plugged his lip with a bolt of teeth-yellowing tobacco.

"Forget Legion."

Past's Second Squad Leader broke over the radio.

"Go for Echo-6," the Staff Sergeant replied.

"Eyes on. Tangoes; Sierra and Whiskey."

"Where?"

"The big culvert. They're setting in. Permission to engage."

"Hold 'til I get there. Out."

The Staff Sergeant traced along his midscale map.

"In fifty kilometers, they're mine."

He folded his chart, face smeared with self-satisfaction.

"Ready or not, Searcher."

6. CURRENTLY

Towering redwood trees supported a blanket of stars. Between their trunks, the narrow path extended into the night.

A culvert, large enough for a man to stand up, crossed under the path.

The wanderer occupied one end of the duct. Kristian reclined in the other, trying in vain to fall asleep.

Evan breathed evenly, as though he slept on feathers.

Kristian shook his head.

How can he sleep when we're in enemy territory, wearing full clothing, and our stomachs are totally empty?

The undulating metal of the pipe pressed into the searcher's bones.

"I'm gonna build a mat from the plants," Kristian had announced a couple hours earlier.

"I wouldn't do that," Evan had said.

You're not the only one who can be right around here, pal.

"I'll be fine," Kristian had replied evenly.

But when he lay on the mattress, the moss sponged moisture out, soaking his clothes.

Kristian was too stubborn to change his situation.

He could have explained it to me, he grumbled.

Might as well keep watch while I'm awake.

He burned through the foliage. A puff of wind stirred the ferny groundcover, but there appeared no cause for concern.

Evan snorted contentedly, and Kris looked towards him, hoping an icy glare would wake his companion.

He turned back to the trees.

A man's form stood out against the backdrop of stars, the toes of his boot just inches from Kristian's face. The searcher jumped.

"Are you a friend?" Kristian sputtered.

The stranger's tall, sinewy frame suited the backdrop of sequoias well. His face twisted with feeling before he spoke.

"You need to go, Kristian. Wake your companion."

The man's voice filled with urgency.

"Now."

Evan stirred, and the movement drew Kristian's gaze. When he looked back outside, the stranger was nowhere to be seen.

Kristian hesitated.

Should I act on the warning of a stranger? I could, but I don't really want to get up.

The woods erupted in a hail of rifle and mortar fire. The humid tang of gunpowder hung on the night air.

Evan leapt to his feet.

"COME ON!" he shouted.

A bullet drilled through Kris's left calf.

Evan pulled Kristian from the rear of the culvert while firing on the ambushers.

Kristian glimpsed Staff Sergeant Past moving between the trees and screaming for his soldiers to advance.

Evan half-dragged and half-carried his battle mate down a creek bed.

Past sprinted to the mouth of the culvert. He clicked the light on his weapon to infrared mode and yanked his night vision goggles over his eyes. The bright blood trail leapt out against the dark green background.

"We bled one of them. IR lights, Platoon on line!"

The three squads transitioned into a wide swath over one hundred meters long. Like a gray broom, the platoon pushed across the path and through the trees on the other side.

Evan pinned Kris against a trunk and worked a combat tourniquet onto his leg.

"You still got that pistol?"

Kris nodded. He opened the double chamber, quickly inspecting the two rounds. At nearly half an inch in diameter, the large .45 ACP round looked formidable. Its hollow point, housed in a smooth brass casing, shone with a deep crimson red.

Evan applied a final twist. Kris's teeth mortar-pestled in pain. The wound stopped bleeding.

Kristian flicked his pistol back together.

"Put your weight on it."

Kris was able to limp. Evan supported him and led him deeper into the forest.

The blood trail thinned away to nothing. Past scanned the area frantically.

"Double time."

A bald redwood, blackened and crunchy from a past wildfire, rose out of the darkness. Evan and Kris collapsed inside its hollow center.

"Find them!" the Staff Sergeant growled.

Craning his neck around the tree, Evan watched as the enemies angled away.

Delirious with shock, Kris asked aloud, "Who is he?"

Evan slapped a hand over Kristian's mouth, but Past snapped towards the voice.

The Staff Sergeant silently motioned his soldiers towards the burnt tree.

With noiseless, precision movements, Evan pulled the pin from a grenade and held the sphere of potential energy to his chest.

The soldiers spread towards the trunk. Staff Sergeant Past pointed to a fire team of four.

"J-hook to the far side," he ordered in a low tone.

The soldiers melted from the line.

Moving around the tree, the front soldier snagged on a vine. As he pulled his heel to kick loose, the Janissaire behind him shouted.

"Wait!"

The leg followed through, displacing a paracord tripwire. The grenade, wedged between the charred wood and the ground, yanked free and percussed.

Spiral, expanding wires dropped the two forward soldiers permanently. The other fire team members fell behind them, wounded.

In the distance, Kris and Evan sprinted to freedom. They rejoined the path further up. Once on it, they ran as best as they could with Kristian's leg. The second grenade that Evan had rigged thumped in the forest behind them.

A signpost announced "City of Currently, eighteen miles."

*****

A no-nonsense knock sounded on the old wood.

Katy Influence opened the door.

Three tactical vehicles shredded the flower beds.

The Lieutenant Colonel and his aide occupied the front porch, their ashy figures starkly contrasting the hanging plants and country swing.

Katy's eyes landed on an open window. Inside the truck a figure hunched in the shadows. Katy recognized the hooked nose. And the clack of knitting needles.

"What's she doing here?" Katy whispered, her throat suddenly tight.

The Lieutenant Colonel moved to block her view.

"We need some time with Christi. Undisturbed."

"I'm not sure I can leave my dear sister alone. Unless..."

The Battalion Commander nodded. Sergeant Major Shame produced a thick glass bottle.

Shame lifted the alcohol to her eyes. Katy snatched it.

"Why don't you go find somewhere quiet to enjoy that?"

Katy hurried off to the barn with her prize as the high-grade soldiers moved into the house.

Christi sat in her corner, but instead of staring into the wall, as was her custom, she carefully studied an object. She held the wedding picture in her lap and traced its lines sentimentally.

It didn't matter that I had a hand-me-down dress. I felt like the most beautiful bride in the world.

She forgot her wheelchair.

He made me feel beautiful.

The Lieutenant Colonel rested a hand on her shoulder.

"Will you let me see that?"

Suddenly aware of the strangers, Christi clutched the frame tightly.

Sergeant Major Shame pulled a vile of REGRET from his assault pack.

"Negative," the Lieutenant Colonel ordered. "This is not an ideal application. It would be ineffective. Bring in the Giant's Wife."

Moments later, the old wretch hobbled into the house. Harsh, clever eyes glinted from deep sockets recessed in her weathered face. Web-necked, rib-thin, and spindle-fingered, the hag looked to be a thousand years old.

"Girl time," the Lieutenant Colonel observed.

He and his counselor sought the outdoors.

The stranger moved behind Christi.

I think I recognize her, Christi thought.

"Who are you?"

The hag shushed her flightless victim.

"You can't see my picture," Christi mumbled.

"I don't want it," the stranger rasped. "But tell me why you should love an abandoner."

Christi's jaw clenched. The hag was no friend of hers, but the words hit their mark.

The Giant's Wife breathed more of the same thoughts until Christi's head began to nod.

A bag made from worn yarn hung on her drooping shoulders. From it, she removed a manila folder.

She slid a yellow fingernail under the paste seal, dry and spackled like her own lips, and produced an image.

Christi's pupils enlarged. Her fingers relaxed from the wedding photograph. The hag stole the vision and replaced it with her own.

Christi's fingers closed on the black and gray. She studied the blurry picture.

The Giant's Wife worked her knitting needles quickly.

*****

The old figure shuffled toward the tactical trucks.

The Lieutenant Colonel spun his vehicle's radio down.

"Well?"

"She's not going anywhere," the hoarse voice answered. "One or two more visits and she'd be his executioner."

The Lieutenant Colonel nodded to his driver.

"Spin 'em up."

The vehicles pulled onto the lonely gravel road.

"What about the wedding photograph?" the Battalion Commander queried.

The hag showed a corner of the stolen image.

"One for my collection."

The driver turned and addressed the BC.

"Where to, sir?"

"City of Currently. Double time. I want to be there by nightfall."

*****

The sun shone brightly. The redwoods gave way to rolling golden hills. As long as one stayed off the ridge, the countless mounds provided excellent cover.

Kristian tightened fresh gauze around his leg as he walked down the path. A toothy stone caught his boot, and pain jolted through the wound.

His pursuer's face came to mind.

"Who is he?"

"He is called Past," Evan responded, anticipating the question.

"Why's he after us?"

"He's a career soldier. Reports directly to the senior officer of the 2nd Psy Ops Battalion, a lieutenant colonel. Past is sent to haunt, to hunt all searchers. If he can't bring them back, the standing order is to kill them."

"Does he ever catch them?"

"He doesn't have the power to detain you."

Across the hills, a city shone. It commanded a strategic view of the wide valley. Evan pointed to it.

"The City of Currently."

Kristian shifted uncomfortably.

"Have you been there before?"

"Many times."

"Is it hostile?"

"You'll get through fine. But I'm going to die there."

*****

The sidewalks sparkled.

The simple yet modern architecture bore the mark of designers influenced by burnished aluminum and snowy silicon.

The city dwellers thronged along crowded streets. Both genders wore their hair long. No men were seen with facial hair.

The mode was thin denim, lobe gauges, and impulse tattoos. Flannel, once worn for its ability to insulate through long winters, now tapered into a slim cut.

As the two foreigners walked against the mass, their appearance drew hateful eyes. Red road dirt stained their clothes. Kristian's crimson beard was now just as full as Evan's.

A woman about Christi's age hugged her son away from the searcher's path. Her eyes held on Kristian untrustingly.

From their alternating shades of plaid, the residents' unkind eyes stabbed into the outstanders.

"Why do they all look the same?" Kristian asked.

Evan hailed a passing boy.

"Tell him why you wear that."

The kid answered with condescension.

"I'm expressing my individuality."

The kid vanished into the crowd of duplicate individuals.

"Who are you, and what were you doing with that boy?"

A tall man with a young face and eyes like a ferret blocked Evan's path.

"I'm Evan, what's your name?"

"I'm not here to make conversation with you," the man hissed. "All you need to know is I speak for everyone here. Why are you dressed different? Where do you come from?"

"I wander all over, sharing good news with others."

"What news?"

"About the King and how—."

"—So you're a radical! A cultist."

The commotion drew a crowd.

"It's not so radical. We are only simple searchers."

The declaration fanned the suspicious watchers into flame.

"They're searchers!" the man shouted.

"Hateful fools!" a woman snarled.

"But we don't hate anyone," Evan said.

"Xenophobe!" they accused.

"Bigot!" someone shouted.

The accusatory cries overwhelmed Evan's volume. The crowd bordered on rioting. The accessories of daily life became ranged weapons.

The swarm closed around the travelers.

Whistles and sirens rose over the angry voices.

A police force flooded the square and formed into a ring around the searchers.

The police chief, a middle-aged man with a handsome mustache, leapt atop a patrol vehicle. A megaphone magnified his presence.

"These men will be tried publicly. If you have a grievance, bring it to the trial. Disperse now."

A fresh wave of police officers circled the crowd with fire hoses.

*****

Hillsides covered in tawny grass blurred together outside the truck windows. A heavy-eyed lance corporal drove the vehicle.

In the passenger seat, Past held a thick folder. He studied a large photograph.

"Evan's longtime associate," the Staff Sergeant mumbled.

"Who's that?" the driver asked.

"A guy named Kasey."

The radioman in the back seat tugged his headset off.

"Staff Sergeant, that was the Det at Currently. They think they got him."

Past dropped the folder.

"Move it!" he shouted to the driver.

"The guy in front of me is taking his time, Staff Sarn't."

The Staff NCO grabbed the driver's neck, digging his fingernails in to emphasize the order. Pearls of black blood oozed from the puncture wounds.

"I said now."

*****

"Why did the police help us?" Kristian whispered.

Evan shrugged. The movement jangled his handcuffs.

A stage ascended in the open-air city center. A crowd numbering thousands filled it. A bailiff paraded Kristian and Evan onto the stage. He began to tear away the wanderer's equipment.

"If they're not against us, they're for us," Evan answered.

"Order!" the Judge commanded.

The Judge's eyes spoke of hatred that had been carefully preserved every day of his thirty-five years. Tattoos enwrapped his sunless skin. A thick coat of gel held his hair in perfect strands.

The bailiff gripped Kristian's pink backpack.

"Leave it," the Judge hissed, "He deserves its weight."

The proceedings began. An endless stream of witnesses accused the outsiders of every possible crime. Many at the stand had never even seen the travelers before.

"But we know their type!" they shouted.

Full of endless patience for the crowd, the Judge accepted every testimony. But he barred even a single syllable of defense from the travelers.

Once the multitude had lathered itself into a rage, the Judge raised his hands.

The shouts quelled to a temporary simmer.

"I've heard every word. I have considered the unthinkable behaviors of these two...miscreants."

He turned to the accused.

"I've seen others like you. Troublemakers. Disruptors.

Bigots."

He conducted the crowd expertly. Every word flared their rage.

"Your belief system is one of exclusion. Our city is for inclusion and tolerance. You are intolerant men. You cannot be permitted to sow your message of hate."

The Judge tightened his fists and his wiry forearms flexed in rage.

"And now we come to the verdict." He moved to address the crowd.

"I have made the only possible decision," he continued. "These men have acted against you, so the people of Currently are free to do justice on them. The one condition is this: once the people have had their fill of stones, blows, and chains, these two searchers must be killed."

"How should we do it?" a frail old man shouted.

"Fire."

The Judge slammed the gavel. The echoing CLACK released the crowd.

But Evan was quicker. He drove his shoulder into the bailiff and commandeered the pistol.

"Run!" Evan commanded.

Kristian tore down a backstreet.

Evan shot the chain from his own handcuffs and

sprinted through the narrow alley after Kristian.

Some policemen joined the throng, but most looked to their chief before acting. He shook his head. The law enforcement officers stood aside as the mob careened after the innocent travelers.

Evan stopped on a narrow dirt strip between two buildings.

Kristian ducked under a tower of scaffolding and ran towards the distant city gate, not observing his friend's halt.

Evan kicked the construction rubble, intending to dislodge a weapon of opportunity. He seized a broken hammer handle.

The forward-most pursuers ran towards him. Evan slammed his weapon into them. They crumpled senseless onto the slick clay.

One rioter rode a stolen police motorcycle. Evan sighted the pistol and squeezed its trigger. The vehicle slid into a hydrant. The escaped water mixed the ground to mud.

The bulk of the crowd now appeared, but no more than four or five could fit across the small alley.

As thousands funneled to a manageable number, Evan trampled down his enemies in battle. He dominated each wave.

But every surge of the antagonists drained his ammunition more. Each strike gashed his wooden club apart.

Within moments, his last bullet expired. His weapon split.

And the mob avalanched.

7. LOSS

Christi wheeled to the door. A woman she barely remembered, Fiona, stood outside with Katy's two sons.

"Where's your sister?"

That's right. She's the woman who lives with Katy's husband.

"Out," Christi answered.

"There's been an accident at the mine. Their father is dead."

She shooed the boys inside.

"They have to live here now."

*****

Kris ran far and fast. He passed through the city gate.

Once he had put a substantial distance between himself and the city, he stopped to catch his breath. He realized

Evan's absence.

His bullet wound hammered in pain.

Guilt hit Kristian.

I'm a coward.

He remembered the first firefight back in Comfort County. Evan had prevailed over eight assailants at the coffee shop.

He was barely trying back then. He'll escape and join me in no time.

Feeling a little better, Kristian tackled the problem of his handcuffs.

A stream bubbled across the path. He submerged his wrists. The water softened the skin and lubricated the metal. Kristian slipped the handcuff from his left wrist, but the other one was too tight to remove. He spied a crevice below the bank, long enough for one man.

The sun hobbled on its last legs. Evan still made no appearance.

Go back. The idea arose in Kristian's gut.

A million contradictions filled his mind. But the thought persisted.

Go back.

As he deliberated, the day fell behind dark curtains.

A band of townsfolk could be heard shouting as they

combed through the woods.

Go back.

Kristian pulled himself to his feet.

"I can't abandon him. I won't."

He avoided capture several times as he retraced his steps.

Soon the heavy city gates rose in front of him. They had been closed for the night.

I have to climb the wall.

Kristian's eyes useless in the darkness, he felt for a handhold.

The gates clattered, and Kris moved behind a tree.

A large group emerged from the city. Light spilled after them. They weren't townspeople; they wore gray-black camouflage.

Janissaires.

At the front walked the cheek-scarred staff non-commissioned officer: Staff Sergeant Past.

Sergeant Major Shame appeared as well. He shoved Evan into the ring of raucous soldiers.

I have to do something, Kristian thought.

But his mind emptied.

Staff Sergeant Past chained the wanderer's hands, then he looked expectantly towards the city.

A figure stepped into the archway, his shadow darkening the assembly.

"Attention on deck!" the Sergeant Major bellowed.

The jovial demeanor abandoned the soldiers. Their bodies snapped to the position of attention.

Staff Sergeant Past shoved the prisoner to the ground. Evan laboriously regained his feet.

The Lieutenant Colonel marched from the city. The night chilled noticeably. Not a whisper, not a breath escaped his terrified subordinates.

Kristian recoiled at the face. The sleek otter hair and harsh flint eyes were a darker black than even the night's own shadows.

"Past's boss," Kristian breathed.

He searched for the name, but Evan had never told him.

The Lieutenant Colonel gripped the captive's collar.

"Call for your searcher."

"He's miles away by now," Evan said.

Past slammed the wanderer to the dirt. Evan pushed himself up once more.

"You defy me?" the Battalion Commander shrieked.

He whiplashed the chain around Evan's neck. Fresh blood matted the prisoner's hair.

The junior soldiers shuffled behind one another, eager to avoid the Lieutenant Colonel's wrath.

Staff Sergeant Past bent close to Evan's ear.

"Remember me, Wanderer?"

Kristian strained to hear. He shifted on the mossy log, and the motion slipped his foot. The noise echoed through the forest.

Past turned.

Kristian froze.

The night sounds seemed to cease, suspended in an embalm of fear.

The Staff Sergeant scanned the darkness. His gaze lingered on Kristian's tree.

Past spoke.

"Come out, searcher."

"I didn't hear anything," the BC said.

"I believe he's out there, sir."

The Lieutenant Colonel motioned to Past. The Staff Sergeant slipped into the undergrowth.

If Kris had been scared before, now his heart fully

drained.

He heard Past moving closer and closer through the ground cover.

On the far side of the path, the black woodland shifted. A silhouette took shape out of the night.

Into view stepped the kitten.

"Staff Sergeant, get out here!" the embarrassed Commander ordered.

How do I know the officer's voice? Kristian wondered. *I can't have met him.*

Past broke from cover.

"There's your sound," the boss scolded, pointing to the ferocious furball.

The cat strolled to the center of the path. There it sat, holding eye contact with Evan.

"Kristian is long gone," the wanderer taunted. "You've failed again."

The Lieutenant Colonel dug his pistol into the back of Evan's head.

"We have you."

*****

A barrage of rain fell outside the narrow cave.

Kristian clawed at his spinning head. Death filled his

mind.

He had been to funerals. He knew that the bodies were just shells. They seemed to bear the faces of his friends and family, but they were emptied of the people he had loved. The bodies contained no remnant of the living personalities.

But watching his friend taken. That was different from a funeral.

Kristian thought back to the trigger-puller's face—the nameless specter tugged at his mind.

He thought back over the scene.

The Lieutenant Colonel holstered his smoking pistol. Sergeant Major Shame entered the city with him.

Past lifted Evan's body over his shoulder, probably to burn it somewhere. The soldiers dispersed in ones and twos. The thick gates crashed closed.

Alone, Kristian staggered forward. He collapsed on the place where Evan had lain.

He stayed in that position for far too long. Eventually, mind choked with vinegar emotions, Kris limped to the cave.

Half dead himself, he slumped into a fitful sleep.

8. GAIN

An impossibly tall peak climbed above the forest.

Kristian dragged his stiff leg forward along the hard path. As before, as always.

He asked himself if the half-light belonged to the rising of the sun or to its going down.

Who knows.

Who cares.

An eerie organ melody faded in and out with the wind.

An old ski lift cranked steadily nearby. Kristian saw no operator, no passengers.

The lift paralleled Kristian's route. Above it, the path narrowed into a goat trail and continued up the vertical mountain.

It seemed like a simple decision.

Kristian stepped into a plastic chair, and it swooped him upward.

A fog bank oozed from the ground and wrapped itself around the rusty lift.

Halfway up the mountain, the cable veered to the left. This was a departure from the true path. The cloud thickened. Terror gripped Kristian. He fought for each breath against the dimensionless billow.

The cable thrummed ominously. The steel threads frayed and unwound.

And the line snapped, dropping Kristian to his death.

*****

The searcher flailed awake. The swollen stream had flooded his shallow cave, and the thick, cold mud sucked heat from his skin.

The tight handcuff chafed his wrist, the wound in his leg throbbed, and the backpack straps ground the open sores on his shoulder painfully.

Kristian could hear multitudes of enemies combing the area for him.

It's over for me. I should stay right here and fade away.

The rain beaded off Kristian's Rifle Manual without soaking into it. The wind gusted up, flipping to a page. Kristian read it:

"A great wind tore the mountains, but the King was

not in the wind. And after the wind an earthquake, but the King was not in the earthquake. And after the earthquake a fire, but the King was not in the fire. And after the fire a still, small voice."

Kristian heard a voice, or a voice's impression, inside his own belly.

You will not die. You will live. And you will find the King.

The words snapped Kristian out of his slump.

The sharp noises of men calling to each other and the baying of hounds pierced the night, moving closer and closer to the searcher's position.

Kristian moved onto the path and stole along it, being careful to keep the handcuff from jingling. He progressed down the path carefully, narrowly avoiding the swinging searchlights that froze the rain.

I could wring water from my bones.

The mud caked onto his heavy work boots. Inside them, blisters rubbed in his spongy skin. Kristian pulled the boots off and threw them away.

He stubbed his big toe on a rock.

Why shouldn't I turn back now?

My house is waiting. I always had enough to eat and a comfortable bed. Almost nobody knows I left. I could go back and everything would be the same.

"That's not true," Kristian answered his mind, "If I go back now, I'll have nothing but answerless questions for the rest of my life. Now that I know, I would never be satisfied in Comfort County."

A patrol intersected his path, and Kristian dropped onto the swampy ground.

What if I passed the King in this storm? I would never know it.

The soldiers moved past, unaware of the searcher at their side.

This wandering will break my back.

The mud coated his backpack with a slimy fondant.

Thunder rolled as Kristian walked into the heart of the storm.

The path heightened; steep granite replaced the flat clay. Soon instead of hiking, Kristian had to scale the sheer rock wall. As he moved higher, he considered the sickening fall below.

One bad handhold would mean death.

His wounded leg gave; his body swung against the slick hillside. Rain streamed down his neck.

"I will not die!" Kristian shouted. "I will find the King!"

Kristian found himself on a plateau. The rain clouds split above him. Unresponsive arms and sweat-soaked clothes faded from his mind.

On a hill far away, stood an old, rugged cross. Two smaller crosses bookended it.

Kristian drew close.

Wind whipped the grass to its knees, and lightning branded the night sky.

A man hung on the middle cross.

The rain assaulted Kristian's body and stirred the dirt below him into muck.

Kristian knelt as he regarded the Prince.

The searcher released the summed desperation of his entire life with four familiar words.

"What can I do?"

From the Prince's bruised forehead fell a single drop of blood. It landed on Kristian's temple. The wind did not dissolve the crimson drop, nor did the rain dilute it. It rested on the searcher's brow, of a higher order than the elements.

The drop slid down Kristian's face. In its place shone clean, bright skin. The drop multiplied as it went. The cleanness spread down Kristian's face and neck. The red moved past the backpack. The plastic buckles dissolved. The burden cratered into the soupy ground.

Kristian's eyes closed.

The brightness reached his arm, opening the handcuff. The open sores on his shoulders healed. The stained dressing fell from the bullet wound. Not a scar remained.

A shine from the ground pulled Kristian's eyes. Light

emanated from a set of golden dog tags.

Kristian scooped them up. A single word stamped the metal: "ALMA."

Whatever dark secrets the backpack had held now became a thing of beauty.

The skies cleared.

"Thank you."

Kristian brought the golden plate to his lips. His face glowed with peace and joy.

*****

Staff Sergeant Past worked the focus on his binoculars. He watched as a storm swirled the distant peak.

"The searcher's with *Him*."

"We can't go up there, Staff Sarn't?"

"I'm not gonna die today."

Past drummed his fingers against the optic.

A soldier approached with a black radio for the staff NCO.

"Higher wants a SitRep, Staff Sarn't."

Past snatched the radio and clicked the volume knob to OFF.

"No."

"But the Colonel said—"

"Maintain radio silence," Past ordered.

The radio operator cocked his head.

"What are you looking at?" Past growled, "Get to your trucks! We're moving."

The driver keyed up the vehicle.

"The searcher has to meet the Immerser after this. We'll skirt the mountains and set in on the far side. Once we take them, I'll give the Colonel his precious SitRep."

Past slammed the truck door.

"I know exactly where the searcher will be."

9. SKILLS

Kristian walked tall as the mountaintop faded behind him. It was a new day.

The path leveled towards oak groves that elbowed out space between natural hayfields. In some places, the golden grass reached shoulder height.

A stranger stood on the path in the cool of the woods. On seeing Kristian, he moved forward.

The man wore familiar coyote-colored gear over his mahogany skin. A brown cap like Evan's rested on his head. A shining .44 Magnum revolver was strapped and canted at chest-height on the man's flak. Kristian felt that the stranger could handle the pistol better than most men could use a rifle.

The man smiled as he approached Kristian.

"You met the Prince. I can tell."

"Evan said there was someone named Ian around here.

Is that you?"

"Ian the Immerser is what they call me," Ian laughed, "though I do not know why. Any man may do what I do. I am happy to meet you."

"I'm Kristian. What do you do?"

Holy mischief twinkled in Ian's brown eyes.

"Come with me."

Kristian followed him down the path. Beside the trail, a stream babbled. Where the land dipped into a natural depression, the flowing waters slowed into a wide pond.

Ian the Immerser walked into the water. It reached to his waist. Kristian joined him.

"Are you ready to die to your old self?"

"Yes."

The Immerser positioned Kristian's body to dunk him.

"Then die with the Prince…"

He submerged the searcher.

"…And rise with the Prince."

As the water flowed off Kristian's face, his eyes caught movement on the bank.

Past and his troops circled the pond.

Kristian looked to Ian, who seemed unruffled.

"You must go," Ian commanded the Janissaires.

"We have nothing to do with you, Immerser. Give us the deserter and we'll be on our way."

"You can't have him."

Ian raised his hand high. With this motion, the pond's water shot into the air.

Kristian looked at his feet. He now stood on dry land.

"You must go," Ian repeated.

He flicked his hand, and the water began to circle the banks like a buzz saw.

"Kill!" Past yelled. The soldiers fired towards the water wall, but the bullets could not penetrate it.

Ian stretched his hand forward, and the water obeyed. It moved faster and faster, catching more soldiers with each turn.

When the Immerser lifted his arms, the water surged and seized the enemies. The Janissaires struggled in vain against the current. Ian struck his arms forward and the water shot downstream, conducting Past and all his soldiers with it.

Delivered from his enemies, Kristian felt a beautiful peace, a smoothness in his soul.

The stream returned to its gurgling.

Ian took the same hands that had commanded the

water and held them over Kristian's chest.

"Let Kingsbreath fill you."

A fire built below Kristian's sternum. His hands tingled. He felt something like fiery tongs moving his tongue. Unknown words fell from Kristian's mouth.

"What is that?"

"A dialect of Kingsland," Ian laughed. "You're glowing."

It was true. Light shone from Kristian's eyes.

"What about Past?"

"He's on the other side of the water."

*****

Kristian projected strength. Rock-face muscle lined his arms. His red-brown hair faded into a full beard. A moisture-wicking combat shirt molded around his cannonball deltoids. Ripstop earth-tone trousers covered his legs. Bare feet gripped the smooth path.

Through the treetops, he saw a peeking white country steeple.

As the oaks opened, Kristian saw a meadow and at the center, a quiet house of worship. Beside the building, a tin shed contained exercise machines.

Inside, a grizzly of a man with a black, flowing beard was covering his hands with chalk. A bar stacked with heavy plates grazed his ankles. The stranger bent down in a deadlift.

He hoisted the 600 pounds.

"You serve the King?" Kristian called to the stranger.

The man dropped the weight. He grabbed his AR-15 and spun around. When he saw Kristian's new clothing, he smiled.

"I do, brother."

The man settled the familiar coyote cap onto his smooth head.

"Who are you?"

"I'm Pastor. Welcome to Beth-Melek."

"What is this place?" Kristian asked.

"The King charged me to build a house for weary travelers. Here they may rest, re-fit, and be supplied with articles of war."

Kristian's muddy feet slipped on the cement floor of the shed.

Pastor steadied the searcher with an arm that engulfed Kristian's shoulder.

I'm glad we're on the same team.

"Let's start with some shoes for you."

Pastor opened a trapdoor below the weight bench. A staircase descended into the dark hole.

He leaned in secretively.

"Maybe some other gear, too."

The stairs led to a sparse cellar. A small library lit by candles covered the far wall.

Pastor pounded the barrier, voice alive with merriment.

"Open up!"

The humble bookshelves slid away, revealing a huge underground chamber lined with concrete and steel.

Endless polished weapons caught the warm light. The gear locker held enough supplies to outfit an army: mounds of body armor, crates of ammunition.

Another searcher zeroed her pistol at the indoor shooting range.

A pretty blonde girl oiled a rifle chamber.

"This is my daughter Hope," the big man explained.

A different girl strapped a magnifying glass over her waterfall curls. Careful fingers threaded ceramic hexagons together with a Kevlar coil.

"And this is my eldest, Faith. Between the three of us, we'll get you outfitted right."

Pastor selected a finely stitched gun belt from a leatherworking table.

"It's hard to be a warrior when your trousers are falling

down." He laid the belt across Kristian's arms.

Pastor chose a woven Kevlar plate carrier. It contoured perfectly to Kristian's body. The flak's network of straps hung with tourniquets, fragmentation grenades, a tactical flashlight, a strap cutter, and a personal first aid kit. The long pouches carried one hundred and eighty rounds of rifle ammunition in six magazines.

Hope brought socks and combat boots for Kristian. They fit like bespoke. He felt that the light footwear would support his ankles under heavy loads but also be weightless enough for running long distances.

Faith showed her skill with the stitched tiles. She had fashioned them into flexible, bullet-resistant plates.

Kristian placed them as inserts into the front, back, and sides of his flak jacket. Between the flak's fabric and the ballistic tile, no .30-06 fiery darts would be able to harm him.

Pastor handed him a ball cap with the same horizontal white cross that all Kristian's advocates had worn.

The load-out was familiar: every article matched Evan's gear. But one item was still absent.

Hope extended a factory-new rifle to the searcher. The weapon, a custom-built AR-15, accepted 5.56x45 millimeter rounds. The rifle's quicksand-colored grip accented the matte black of its barrel. A fiber optic-powered Trijicon scope crowned the rail.

Kristian noted the rifle's manufacturer as he accepted the weapon solemnly: LOGOS Arms.

"I don't really know how to shoot."

"It's all right. You're in the right place," Pastor laughed.

They spent the next months in training. In between rifle drills, Pastor explained the manual. What it meant, how to wage war. How to win.

And Kristian became deadly with every weapon.

*****

Staff Sergeant Past hacked sand from his tender lungs.

Body bruised, he painfully elbowed himself up. He searched the sand bar. Many gray-clad figures lined the shore, unmoving.

Past worked up and down the bank, checking each body. Soon, his fear was confirmed.

His entire platoon. Destroyed.

Past had failed to apprehend the searcher.

He had failed his mission.

*****

Kristian exited the steepled refuge a new man.

Pastor strode next to him.

"I am sorry to see you go, but I know you must leave."

"I'm worried I've spent too much time here already."

"I have a parting gift for you."

Pastor extended a bundle. From it, Kristian pulled a sand-colored Nimravus blade and a drop holster carrying a Sig Pro 2022. Stamped letters bragged the pistol's chamber size: 9mm *Para*.

"What's 'Para'?" Kristian asked as he examined the gift.

Pastor took the weapon.

"Parabellum, from an old language, Si vis pacem, para bellum: If you want peace, prepare for war."

Pastor held the slide back.

"Dark places line the road ahead, Kristian."

He transferred the pistol to Kristian. The searcher seated a round in the chamber and holstered the decocked weapon.

"Staff Sergeant Past is known to you. You don't need to fear him. But there are reports of another enemy in the area, elements of the Stress Division. They use harassing attacks. Be vigilant."

Kristian nodded. He performed one final gear check.

"I want to go with you," Pastor admitted, "But my mission doesn't take me from here. Yet."

He wrapped Kristian in a strong embrace.

"You will live to see the King."

"Thank you, Pastor. You're a true friend."

Kristian charged the rifle and watched bright brass fill its chamber.

With gloved hand on the pistol grip, Kristian patrolled towards the horizon, adventure-hungry and combat-ready.

10. ALLIED

"Where is he?"

"Past, sir?" the Sergeant Major responded.

The two top soldiers inspected a line of men and women. Chains held them. Some prisoners wore the cap of the searchers. One particularly burly man named Tom Resilient held his chin in defiance.

"We've been busy, you and I, but it's been weeks since his last SitRep," the Lieutenant Colonel said.

"I can try to raise him with comm."

"We can't wait any longer. Find him."

*****

Thorn bushes choked the path. Though they clawed at Kristian's Camelbak, they could not pull his spirit down.

The briars gave way to a rising hill.

Kristian felt a strong sense of déjà vu.

A creepy calliope faded up with the breeze.

Clinking mechanically to his left, a real version of the ski lift turned.

A grungy shack sheltered the machine's gears. Its sign read, "The Real You."

Kristian pulled the pin from a grenade and pushed it through a window.

As the fuze wound down, Kristian joined the slender upward path.

Maybe this won't be so hard.

*****

The path moved across the mountain's side. On the right, the slope continued upwards beyond the treeline. A waist-high stone wall protected travelers from the fall on the left side of the path.

Automatic gunfire cut through the air.

Kristian recognized the guttural bark of the AK-47s.

Enemies. Ten weapons or more. But they're not firing in my direction.

He moved into the treeline to recon the battle.

Around the next bend, he witnessed a one-sided conflict.

Thirteen enemies soldiers shot down towards the path. A solitary man, dressed in the same uniform as Kristian, was firing up from the wall. He knelt mere inches above the deadly drop-off.

Kristian didn't think twice. He chamber-checked his pistol, switched his rifle to SEMI, and milked two grenades.

Hurling the frags, he opened fire.

The enemy had no time to organize: panic seized them.

One foe managed to get a shot off, and the round crumpled against Kristian's body armor. The blow angered him.

As soon as his magazine ran dry, Kristian took up his pistol.

Fallen enemies tumbled down the hillside. The second searcher increased his rate of fire on the distracted ambushers. His shots landed with surgical precision.

When the Sig Pro clicked empty, Kristian pulled out his knife.

The five remaining enemies turned to flee. Four fell under the rescued searcher's sights.

Kristian threw his knife, and it plunged into the final enemy.

Breathless, the rescued man stepped over the wall. He stood the same height as Kristian, but his frame was stockier. Dark brown facial hair crowded around his mouth.

"I don't think 'thank you' sums it up."

"Anybody would have done the same," Kristian replied, moving down to shake the stranger's hand.

"Name's Jack, Jack Consistence. Those Stress Division 'Jannies' have been tailing me for weeks. Trying to stop my progress towards the King."

"We have the same destination then."

Jack nodded as he tucked a worn brown shemagh into his flak jacket.

"We should travel together."

Happy to have a companion once more, Kristian became fast friends with Jack.

During their journeys through the soaring mountain passes, the searchers exchanged tales of failures and firefights. And the traveling became a little easier.

*****

A wide road gashed through the forest of southern pines. A carpet of gray needles spread over the ground. Signs fastened to tree trunks advised that this Main Supply Route was maintained and patrolled by elements of the 2nd Psy Ops Battalion. The signs pointed east towards Battalion Headquarters.

Staff Sergeant Past limped west.

"I will kill that searcher."

Rumbling vehicles appeared on the hill to the front.

Weaponless, Past labored off the trail. But not in time.

Military police streamed from the trucks.

Past tried to run, but the soldiers brought him down easily.

Sergeant Major Shame stepped out.

Approaching the struggling Staff Sergeant, the advisor's mouth twisted into a wicked smile.

"BC wants to see you."

*****

"How's your ammo?" Consistence asked.

Kristian filed through his magazines.

"I could use a top off," he replied.

The path seemed to wind through the mountains endlessly.

"There has to be an ammunition supply point somewhere."

Olive ammo cans appeared on the side of the road.

As the men approached the boxes, the lids lifted. Inside, a welcome assortment awaited. 9-mil mags, boxes of 5.56, grenades, and chem sticks. The men stuffed the pouches of their Camelbaks.

A long silicone sleeve lay behind the cans. The tag read simply, "For Consistence."

Jack pulled out a weapon: The HK416 rifle. It looked like an AR-15. However, the HK leveraged a piston-driven system; thousands of rounds would cycle through it before the carbon buildup choked its operation.

Kristian wanted one. Jealousy crept into his heart. But he faked a smile and called it wonderful.

*****

Staff Sergeant Past stood with arms locked to his body and eyes fixed on the horizon. Dry mud cracked on his ragged uniform.

The Lieutenant Colonel stormed around him.

"You had weeks to find and capture him!"

"Sir, I did find him," Past hissed. "Three times."

"You failed me three times. I gave you forty bodies against two men. What's that ratio, Sergeant Major?"

"Twenty to one, sir," Shame said.

"So where's the platoon I gave you?"

"Gone," Past answered.

"Destroyed!"

"Sir, he always had help. It's not my fault—"

The responsibility-devoid words triggered the Lieutenant Colonel. He upended a table and charged the Staff Sergeant.

The Commander gouged his fingertips into Past's eyes.

*****

Thin pines encircled a small lake. The clouds drew back to reveal an almond-sliver moon.

As Kristian built a fire belowground, his companion busied himself with water purification.

Jack unslung his HK and sat against a tree.

Once the fire crackled, Kristian leaned back to clean his weapon.

Jack doesn't have to bust any carbon off his nice, new rifle.

In between pumping the water filter, Jack's fingers moved back and forth across the shemagh. His lips worked inaudibly in time with the motion.

As Kristian disassembled his rifle and brushed it free of carbon and road dust, he noticed Jack's behavior.

"What are you doing?"

"Oh. I'm studying a codex."

"The scarf?"

"The scarf," Jack laughed. "Long ago, when I had the Rifle Manual in front of me, I attached words to each thread in my mind. A line of cloth for a line of text. I memorized every knot and snag. This frayed bit here starts with, 'Faith is the down payment of the yet-unseen.'"

"You have the whole book memorized?"

"I have the *words* memorized. I'm still working out how to live them. I could tell you stories of men slaying giants verbatim or of dead ones raised as though from sleep."

Consistence's eyes searched the fire.

"But I fear my weak faith will be my downfall."

"Maybe not," Kristian said.

Jack smiled.

"Enough about me. Tell me more about your wife."

Kristian gave his weapon a functions check as he considered how to respond.

"I miss her. Not who she decided to be in that wheelchair. I want the love we used to have. The young kind. But I think she'll hate me forever."

"The King specializes in restoration, so…maybe not."

*****

The Lieutenant Colonel's pale knuckles gripped the table. Slowly, his terrifying fire eyes softened to stone. The bony fingers smoothed his hair.

"Want me to finish him?" the Sergeant Major said.

"No. Past is the least of my worries. Move him from

the brig to the dungeon until I decide what to do with him."

A guard entered.

"Sir, a man is here. He says he has an appointment."

"Bring him."

A portly man entered the tent. He moved to shake the Lieutenant Colonel's hand.

"How are things, Colonel?"

"Grim."

The BC turned to his aide.

"Sergeant Major, this is Bill Turned. One of my first projects. He started as a searcher."

"That was a long time ago, sir."

"What could you possibly do for us, 'Bill'?" the Sergeant Major sneered.

The smooth face spread into a joyless smile.

"It's 'Mayor' to enlisted soldiers, Sergeant Major. I run the city of TomorroWeDie, the largest municipality in the region. Their so-called path runs straight through it."

"There's no margin of error on this one," the boss warned.

"If he's avoided capture for this long, then a fight isn't the right tactic. I assume you want him alive, as always?"

"They make better examples that way."

"It will be simple to take him. They tend to lose vigilance this far along. It's likely that petty things will have already started to break his focus."

The ugly mayor leaned into the red light.

"He will be your prisoner tomorrow."

"He'd better be. Because if we can't get him within the week, we'll have to kill someone else in that square."

"Who?"

"The wife."

11. TWD

Inside a rough brig, Past regained consciousness. His fingers traced his now-useless eyes.

On realizing his blindness, Past's body thrashed. He accidentally kicked his cellmate.

"Watch your big feet," the other soldier said.

"You really gonna talk to a Staff Sergeant like that?" Past barked.

The cellmate laughed.

"All of us prisoners lose rank. You're an E-1 now, 'Staff Sergeant'."

Blind Past seized his mocker.

"I will find him!" he screamed as he beat the soldier.

"I will kill him."

*****

The fifteen-year old burst into the farmhouse. Sage's hands overflowed with ripe wild blackberries. He flew past his older brother, who was occupied with video games.

Sage dropped the berries into a bowl.

She hasn't gotten out of bed for days. Did she ever find the picture?

He knocked on Christi's bedroom door softly.

No answer.

"Aunt Christi, I found some blackberries. Your favorite, remember?"

"She doesn't care," his older brother said.

Sage pushed into the room.

Christi sat propped up in bed, her lips moving without sound.

On Sage's entrance, she didn't even turn. Her lips never stopped moving, and her eyes never left the picture in her hands.

The boy crossed the room with hesitation.

That's not her wedding photo. What is it?

As Sage neared, the picture took shape.

His fingers released the ceramic bowl and it shattered on the floor.

Sage collapsed onto Christi's shoulders, his tears wetting her hair.

Now near her neck, he heard what the thin voice repeated endlessly,

"I hate him I hate him I hate him I hate him I hate him I hate him I hate him…"

*****

Night began to fade into morning. A pothole jolted the truck. Sergeant Major Shame moved with the road bumps, accustomed to the rough suspension of the tactical vehicle.

He tapped the map thoughtfully, right where a circle showed the destination:

Comfort County.

*****

An early glow announced the dawn. Kristian hiked away from the coals. Jack traced behind him.

The forested mountains ended, giving way to wide views. A huge city loomed in the distance. The land fell away behind it. A signpost read, "TomorroWeDie".

Evan's bruised face came back to Kristian's mind.

"Let's go around, Jack."

Consistence shook his head.

"The path leads through it. That's the way we have to

go."

"We could at least disguise ourselves."

"Are you serious?"

"No," Kristian answered, but his heartbeat increased.

The lonely figures soon approached the concrete walls. Iron gates towered above them. A sign announced that they stood open all day and night.

A cold wind howled through the empty streets.

"This isn't right," Jack said, shivering.

A figure appeared at a doorway behind the men.

"Welcome to TWD, friends."

The searchers snapped their sights onto the speaker.

"Who are you?" Kristian asked.

The man smiled.

"Call me Bill."

12. SNARED

"Relax, boys. I'm a friend," the mayor said.

Kristian lowered his rifle.

"I run this place," Bill continued. "And I would like to welcome you with a drink."

"We can't stop," Consistence answered.

"I understand your journey perfectly. I came from that direction myself."

"Then you know we have to keep moving."

"I know when I started, there was no rule for when and where you stopped. Has that changed?"

"No," Kristian admitted.

"Look at how far you've come, how much you've achieved. You can stop for a moment to celebrate."

Kristian nodded to Consistence. The sharp mayor caught the exchange. Turning to Jack, the fat man spoke.

"Unless you care more for yourself than for your friend."

The accusation broke Jack's concentration.

"All right," he conceded. "Then we move."

They followed the mayor inside a bar. Several old men filled it, bloated and beardless.

The mayor sat the boys down at a table and went to order drinks.

Jack left to have a look around.

"Well, hello."

The voice behind Kristian was silk.

Dark hair tumbled her shoulders. She wore a long dress that flowed around high heels. Her beauty was almost paralyzing.

"Hi."

Kristian fought the butterflies.

I shouldn't allow them...but the attention is kind of nice...

"Buy me a drink?" she cooed.

It's not wrong to talk to her.

"I didn't bring any cash."

"Then stay in town and work a while."

"What's your name?"

"Maybe I'll tell you later," she flirted.

Her fingers grazed his, and Kris didn't move his hand away. She smiled and walked off.

Jack grabbed him.

"What?" Kristian snapped, guilt transforming into anger.

"You gotta see this."

He pulled Kristian towards a back room.

The bar games that filled the space—billiards and darts—went ignored. A large crowd gathered at the back.

They surrounded a young man. He appeared to be only nineteen. A patchy beard met the boy's tan baseball cap.

The crowd jostled him. They shouted without any joy on their faces.

"Live for today," a woman called out. "This is all we have."

"Tomorrow we die!" The words rose into a chant.

"Who is he?" Kristian asked.

"Name's Abel Pressured," Jack answered. "I met him a couple of minutes ago. He's one of us."

Abel removed the cross cap. He pulled the patch and stomped the hat. He allowed the onlookers to tear away his articles of war.

A girl grabbed a knife. Caressing Abel's face, she whispered something to him. The boy nodded. Her quick strokes cut away his beard.

Abel, now smooth-faced, drove the knife through the patch and into the wall.

Thousands of similar patches covered the room.

The mayor breathed into Kristian's ear. "When men tire of searching, they come here. These were all searchers once, like you and I."

Jack checked his weapon. "We're going."

"I'm right behind you," Kristian mumbled.

Consistence exited the bar.

The mayor gripped Kristian's shoulder. "You can find love here. Many men do."

I've never seen anyone like her.

What would it hurt to get her name?

Kristian turned back to the bar. He hastily scribbled on a napkin then handed the note to the mayor.

"When that girl comes back, give her this."

"Stay a bit and give it to her yourself."

Kristian considered the proposal.

I could stay here forever. But then I'd never see the King.

He grabbed his rifle and sulkily went out the door.

Bill plucked a radio from behind the bar. Triumph spread across his fat cheeks.

He studied the note and keyed his handset.

"He took our bait."

*****

A gray line of vehicles snaked up and down the chalky hills. In one of them, Past rode as a passenger. His hands were bound. A bandage wrapped both eyes.

The radio crackled.

"He took our bait," the mayor transmitted.

Past's lips curled back from his teeth.

"See you soon, Searcher," he said, malice choking out the words.

*****

Sergeant Major Shame stood at the ready, a veteran war dog in his element. He motioned the troops silently forward. They surrounded the sleeping farmhouse.

Shame's boots slid over the flowerbeds where the tactical trucks had parked on the last visit.

A radio operator crept up and whispered to him.

"Transmission from the Boss, Sergeant Major."

Shame grabbed the handset.

"Sir?" he said in a whisper.

"Sergeant Major, forget the girl. Get back to the Battalion strong point now. He's about to walk into our hands and I want you there when he does."

*****

Kristian and Jack patrolled to the far edge of town, departing unopposed.

The fading sun painted the lush valley in glorious tones.

The path approached a thick forest.

"Some good cover," Jack said.

"And more thorns," Kristian muttered.

Kristian avoided Jack's inquiring eyes.

As they entered the forest, the searchers raised their rifles simultaneously. The woods felt unsafe.

A greenish fog wrapped around the oaks enchantingly. The gaps between the knobby branches tightened, cutting off the last light of day.

The Nameless Woman emerged from the forest.

Her eyes held on Kristian.

He dropped his weapon. It slung loosely on his back, out of reach.

On her body fell a sequined evening gown. Her hand clutched an expensive purse, branded, JUST LOOK.

Consistence tabbed the safety selector on his rifle. Kristian pushed Jack's weapon down.

Kristian tracked her gaze, building the fire in his ribs.

She smiled coyly then glided towards the treeline, stopping to call Kris.

"Aren't you coming?"

She held the napkin with Kris's hurried writing.

She likes me.

She disappeared into the woods, and Kristian moved to follow.

"What are you doing?" Jack asked, surprised.

"I'm gonna recon the area."

"We can't leave the path."

"It's just two steps."

Jack grabbed Kristian's arm and barred the way.

"You're a married man, your wife—"

"What do you know about her? She doesn't love me. She'll never love me."

"There can be restoration—"

"You think you're better than me just cause you got a new rifle?"

"What are you talking about?"

"I'm not gonna sit here and be lectured by someone without the faith to lace up his own boots."

Kristian shoved his friend aside.

Jack called after him.

"Don't do it, Kristian. We're close to the King. I know it!"

Kristian plunged into the forest.

I have to catch her.

He scanned the woods.

I'll get to know her a little. That won't hurt anything.

Kristian caught a glimpse of the woman; she moved quickly. He followed her deep into the forest as night fell. If he hadn't been focused on the pursuit, he would have noticed the letters on her handbag. Instead of *JUST LOOK*, they rearranged and faded so that the brand now read *LUST*.

The deformed trees hid her. Kristian turned in a circle. The forest would not yield any clues about her location.

Every direction looked the same.

A different girl with alluring red hair stepped into view. She was less attractive than the brunette, but she dressed flashily. Excessive makeup caked her face. A headband threaded between her tiger curls. It read simply, PORN.

She, too, stepped away. Kristian pursued, but she was soon lost to the deep forest.

"I will never find someone who loves me," Kris lamented.

A blonde stepped past him. She was the least attractive of the three. She carried some extra weight. The back of her yoga pants read CHEAT.

She touched Kris's face. "I really care for you," she said.

He allowed himself to feel attracted to her.

She disappeared through a wall of thorns.

Slipping his wedding ring into his pocket, Kristian pushed into the underbrush. He didn't notice when a branch snagged his rifle's magazine release, or when his ammo fell into the mud.

He pursued the she-fiend deeper until clawing vines blocked his vision.

The branches lessened in one area, and he rushed towards the clearing.

Though darkness had fallen, a steady wind told him he was in a field.

As he turned to look for the females, his feet crunched on something. He snapped a chem stick to illuminate the object.

A femur.

He raised the light and realized that he now stood in a field of ten thousand skeletons.

Each exhibited a different level of decay, as though they'd been lured and killed here one-by-one, and not as one great army.

The searcher turned to the forest.

CLINK. Something mechanical broke beneath the dirt.

Kris fumbled for his rifle.

And the land mine exploded.

13. PAST

Kristian felt suspended.

His klaxoning head and fresh wounds reassured him that he lived. Fresh cuts marked his agonized face. His left arm twisted painfully, broken. Burns ulcered his skin.

Where am I?

He studied the dark walls. Stone. A window lumined his view. Bars. He sought his rifle. Gone.

Kristian still wore his trousers and shirt, but he was missing his combat load-out.

His brow fell into his hand.

The rifle manual sat on the end of the stone bench, but Kristian turned away from it.

A noise like fingernails on stone came through a hole in the wall behind him.

"Are you awake, searcher?"

It was the voice of Staff Sergeant Past.

"Past, Where am I?"

The blind soldier's own chains rattled as he wriggled closer to the gap.

"You have made yourself his prisoner, you fool."

"How long have I been here?"

"He will torture you. But that won't save you from me. I will get loose, and I will kill you."

What have I done? Kristian despaired.

His eyes landed on an object, and his heart fell. Unable to move, he lay still, staring at it miserably.

On the stone floor, slumped over and lit in the cold light of the dungeon, sat the pink backpack.

From that moment on, Past did not cease to recount Kristian's failures.

As Kristian's painful wounds transferred him in and out of consciousness, he began to accept his failures as the things that defined him.

The days that followed were a febrile fade. Sergeant Major Shame prepared REGRET in lethal doses. He cocktailed other chemicals, SELF-LOATHING, LOW ESTEEM, and more into Kristian's system.

"How is he responding to the medicine?"

The voice of the Lieutenant Colonel broke the current of Kristian's dreams.

"Accepting treatment, sir. We hid most of his equipment, but anyone who touched the Book or his gold relics was severely burned."

"The gold items are precious to the King. I'm surprised you didn't know that. It doesn't matter because the searcher is in no condition to use them. Once we have had our fun with him, we'll transfer him back to Comfort for his execution."

The Lieutenant Colonel bent to Kristian's comatose face.

"Look at you. Weak."

He whispered into Kristian's mind.

"Your wife hates you. And she has every right. It was all your fault. You are a failure."

Kristian flinched.

"Everything is your fault."

Though unconscious, Kristian's hand stretched toward the backpack. His mind replayed the beginnings of his problems.

*****

"Where is the actual gem?" The photographer huffed, "That's the smallest diamond I've ever seen."

Kristian laughed, as did his priceless new wife, but the words wounded him.

The teens tripped down the sidewalk together. Linked elbows stole their balance, pretensing them into each other's arms. Kris examined her ring.

"You deserve so much more. I'll get you the biggest diamond ever, Wildflower."

"You're all I want," young Christi beamed. She held her ring up like a diamond glove.

Kristian shook his head.

"I'll make sure you have everything you ever wanted."

*****

"Don't you have any sense?" Kris's Uncle Avery shouted.

"How long have you worked for me?"

"Since I got married," the twenty-one year old replied. "So three years."

"And you never learned a thing. Cause you don't care."

The truth was Kris worked harder than Uncle Avery, constantly putting in eighteen-hour days on the farm.

But a blight had returned to the land.

"The east pasture was your responsibility."

The night before, Kris had wrenched dead cornstalks

from the soil. He worked beyond sunrise the next day.

Finally, satisfied he'd saved half the crop, he collapsed into a furrow to sleep. He awoke to Avery's shouts. Every single plant had rotted on the stalk.

"I'm not paying you for this week," his uncle announced.

"You're useless. Now I know why your parents left. What I can't figure out is why that girl stays with a loser like you."

*****

Kris made sure to never bring up their poverty, but he searched every conversation with his wife for possible accusations.

Tonight, he felt like the walls of the tiny apartment were closing in. The flowery wallpaper that had been so hysterically tacky when they first moved in now threatened to crush him.

"I made veggie lentils again," Christi smiled.

Kris heard it as a complaint.

"What did you mean by that?"

"Dinner is ready, crazy."

She's lying. She hates your pitiful paycheck. And guess what? You don't even have that this week.

*****

Kris fought two simultaneous battles: He beat against the wildfire and he wrestled with exhaustion.

Avery engaged the orange circle at Kris's back. The fire had already consumed all the crops and equipment on the two hundred-acre farm. The two men fought tooth and nail to save the old farmhouse.

The uncle collapsed.

After Kris pounded out the flame's final licks, he rushed to Avery's side.

"Everything's gone," the man choked. "I can't pay my debts. You've ruined me."

He repeated those words to Kris for the next three weeks. They were the last words Avery said before he died of smoke inhalation.

*****

The lawyer summarized the uncle's will on the phone.

"In other words, you inherited his substantial debts."

Kris gripped the receiver.

Don't tell her. Carry it all yourself. You're not providing for her. If you tell her, she'll finally know that you're not a real man.

Kris spent the whole day trudging around the city. His thoughts tormented him. He intentionally stayed away from home until he knew his wife would be asleep.

He snuck into the dark apartment.

A covered bowl sat on the table. He picked up the towel over it.

Lentils. Of course.

As he washed his face, he noticed the wastebasket. A blue-white stick poked from it.

Pregnancy test.

Christi woke to a bowl smashing against the wall.

"You want a baby? We can't afford two people and you want a baby?" Kris screamed.

"I thought you'd be happy."

"Well, I'm not! We're not having it."

"Her," Christi uttered quietly.

*****

The lawyer suggested a clinic that did this type of thing for almost no cost.

Kris drove her there on a Friday. While they operated, he worked on papers to sell off most of the property.

*****

The discount doctor called the next day.

"In many cases, the mother exercises the option for an unrestricted life now, but the procedure may limit her ability to produce in the future. Do you understand?"

He paused to let the words sink in.

"Christi will never bear children again."

*****

Christi moved around the apartment as if in a trance. She pushed anything related to babies into a black trash bag and threw it into the backyard.

Then she occupied the living room corner.

Every time Kris walked in, her jaw tightened, her eyes filled with tears. She wanted nothing to do with the man who took everything from her.

She sat in the corner and wallowed in hatred for the man who had hurt her.

And her muscles atrophied.

Katy brought over a cane one day. As Christi's body weakened, she began to use it. She became less and less active, and a walker eventually replaced the cane. Then came the wheelchair.

Every time Katy visited, she echoed what Kris and his wife already held to be true:

That everything was his fault.

*****

He rustled through the black trash bag. Guilt pulled at Kris like a burden.

He pulled the rose-pink backpack from the trash and pawed the baby accessories into it.

I'll carry this sin forever.

A name book fell open. On the page, a scribbled pink heart highlighted a name:

ALMA.

14. RECLAIMED

Maggots wriggled around Kristian's dead skin. His broken arm torqued in pain.

The REGRET flexed inside him.

"What can I do?" Kristian begged the night.

A voice cut through the air above him.

"Roll onto your back."

Kristian fought the idea.

"Give me something real to do."

"Roll onto your back," the voice repeated.

Kristian opposed the words, but they persisted.

If I ever want peace, I have to do it.

Kristian half-rolled. He stifled a cry and went back to

his side.

It's the only word I have. I have to try again.

He wrenched his tender body onto his back. Two types of pain speared into him. The first was from his wounds. The other surprised him.

It dug into his lower back in a dull throb.

The master key!

Kristian pored over the pistol. For the first time, he noted an inscription on the side: "ROMEO 8-1".

Kristian opened his dusty manual.

Text projected on the air in golden letters. "There is no Condemnation for Prince-finders."

Kristian repeated the words. He felt the poison's grip on his heart release. He spoke it out again. "There is no Condemnation for Prince-finders."

His soul lightened.

Over the next days, as he repeated the words to himself, his wounds closed and his bones set.

He tested his left arm by gripping the pistol.

Painless.

"I'm going to escape," he said.

A light cut through the darkness.

It was Grace.

"Dear Kristian, this will help." She smiled and produced his rifle.

She turned to leave.

"Wait."

He pointed to the backpack.

Grace lifted the object and hid it in her clothes.

"I killed her," Kristian confessed.

"Alma was given to you as a gift. Anything that tries to make her a burden is a lie."

"What if the King calls me a baby killer?"

"He has already canceled your sin, so He will only call you by your right name."

Kristian's entire being released the guilt like an exhale. He lifted the golden dog tags.

When he looked up, he stood alone in the cell.

His tactical gear was neatly folded where Grace had stood. He put it on swiftly.

Kristian stepped silently to the door, peering through the bars.

The guard slept on duty.

Kristian reached for his key. He bunched his shirt to

muffle the shot.

Lifting Alma's golden name to his lips, he kissed it. He put his wedding ring back where it belonged.

Hammering the pistol back, he said a silent prayer and applied pressure to the trigger.

15. FREE

The lock exploded to splinters.

The noise roused the jailer, but Kristian easily overpowered him.

Past screamed from his cell. "Searcher, release me! You're nothing without me!"

"You're looking for a dead man," Kristian said.

He slammed his rifle stock and knocked Past senseless.

Looking down the hall, Kristian saw several other cells. He opened each one. Most of them held searchers, eight men and three women. The group gladly joined Kristian's ranks.

"Was anyone conscious when they were brought here?" Kristian asked.

The prisoner named Resilient raised his hand.

"Show us the layout, brother," Kristian said.

The man knelt to the dusty floor and traced an outline of the compound.

"The motor pool is over on the west part of the complex. This circle is the Commander's office."

"The Lieutenant Colonel is here?"

"He whispered in your cell while you slept."

"Then it's time to end it. Where's the path from here?"

The man drew a line from the main gate.

"Cross the Boneyard then trace the forest east until it breaks. There's a large body of water further up the path. I'm not sure what to do from there."

Kristian distributed the jailer's weapons.

"Roger. You all take the motor pool," Kristian planned, "Grab a couple of vics. I'll meet you in fifteen."

Kristian left the searchers to make a hasty plan of attack. He climbed a staircase.

An imposing double door stood at the end of the hall.

This is it.

Kristian cracked it open. Sergeant Major Shame and his Commander studied a map.

Kristian pushed into the room.

The Lieutenant Colonel's face registered confusion for a moment before he reestablished his bearing.

"Hello, Kris."

"Who are you?" Kristian demanded.

The Lieutenant Colonel's face twisted hatefully.

"You really don't recognize me? I've talked to you for years."

That voice.

"What is your name?"

"You won't leave here alive—"

"What is your name?"

"—So I will tell you my name. But first, five hundred of my Janissaires occupy this base. So put your gun down. If you touch me, they will tear you apart."

Kristian shoved his rifle into the officer's neck.

"What. Is. Your. Name?"

The Sergeant Major glanced to his pistol, just out of reach on the table.

The Battalion Commanding Officer stood up.

"I am Lieutenant Colonel Condemnation."

Kristian suddenly knew the voice. It flashed into every moment of self-doubt in his entire life—his uncle, Alma, and his recent failures on the path. It was Condemnation who had tortured Kristian for destroying the child, and it was Condemnation who had kept Kristian from making things right with Christi.

"You?"

"You believed anything I ever said to you. You care too much. It makes you weak. And that's why you will never, ever escape me."

Sergeant Major Shame eased towards his pistol.

"Do you really think the King wants a baby killer like you?"

Condemnation pressed his advantage.

"Alma," his sick mouth smirked.

Kristian didn't debate with the fiend; he only quoted from the Rifle Manual.

"There is no Condemna—"

The Sergeant Major seized his weapon. He fired before Kristian could react, and the shot grazed Kristian's left arm. It was the last thing Shame ever did.

Kristian rocketed back into the hallway, firing as he went.

A fire team poked into the Lieutenant Colonel's office.

"FIND HIM!" Condemnation screamed.

Kristian flew down the hall. Rounding a corner, he

collided into someone: Jack Consistence.

"Jack! What are you doing here?"

"You know I couldn't abandon a brother."

Shots rang out. Enemy soldiers spilled from the doorways. The two men took off running.

A guard tried to bayonet Jack, but Kristian knifed him.

"Hey, about earlier—"

Two soldiers ran up. Kristian and Consistence pulled their triggers at the same instant.

"It never happened," Jack said as he knocked down a new enemy.

"What's the plan?" he shouted.

"Lead the prisoners out, get back on the path," Kristian said.

"Good. Then I'll find some backup."

Consistence turned off the main corridor. Enemy bullets smashed the walls behind him.

Kristian tore through the passage. To his front, the hall opened on the motor pool. Enemy bodies covered the ground. The free searchers filled two tactical trucks.

Kristian ran up, shouting, "Spin 'em up!"

The mob of Janissaires pursued him.

The stolen vehicles rolled away, and Kristian jumped into the forward one. Liberated rifles returned fire on the gray soldiers.

The searchers plowed the gate to freedom.

Once past the Boneyard, the two vehicles sped across the plains, making for the forest. Just as the prisoner had predicted, a huge sea shimmered on the horizon.

The treeline broke ahead. The thin red path became visible beyond it.

"Bear right," Kristian ordered.

An enemy mortar shell impacted the ground.

DOONKT!

A full mortar salvo followed, and the earth trembled. The explosions churned the dirt into spikes. New craters blocked the way to the path.

"Make for the water! It's our only shot!" Kristian commanded.

A wall of dust rose behind the escaping searchers.

"Contact rear!" someone shouted. "Enemy vics inbound!"

Thirty troop carriers, ten gun trucks, and a tank raced over the ground towards the searchers.

A mortar shell cut between Kristian's two trucks. One of the drivers spun the wheel too late, and the vehicle crashed into the crater. Six searchers streamed out.

"Spin it around," Kristian commanded his driver.

After a quick turn, Kristian's truck screeched to a halt next to the crash.

Everyone dismounted and fired on the closing enemies.

The mortar impacts bracketed closer and closer to the men.

"How are we on ammo?" Kristian's voice roared above the din.

"On our last mags!"

Kristian grasped for a plan.

The ocean limits our advance.

The tank main gun fired. Shot from the move, the shell landed short.

One hit will wipe us out.

A second tank rolled in behind the Janissaire force. The Lieutenant Colonel commanded it.

He screamed into the radio, "Shoot the gunner in Tank One! Elevate your barrels now and shut those mortars down! I want him alive."

The tanks raised their guns, and the mortars fell off.

Kristian's squad prepared for close combat. Some of them grabbed stones. Some fixed bayonets. Tom Resilient grabbed two mirror shards to use as daggers.

"Let's go," he said.

The enemy moved into a half-moon around the men and women. The gray Janissaires dismounted and placed their sights over Kristian's squad.

Enemy on three sides and water to the rear.

We're trapped.

Twelve heartbeats hammered out the seconds.

*****

Several minutes earlier, Jack threaded through the castle, ascending staircases, gunning down enemies without pausing, changing mags like a machine.

He approached the roof. The enemy's mortar position stood atop the fortress. From there they fired on any escaped searchers.

When they saw Jack, the mortar team hit the deck. They popped their heads above sandbags to fire their carbines at him.

Jack rolled an incendiary grenade towards the stack of mortar ammunition.

He leapt from the roof to avoid the explosion.

Looking up, he found himself in the Boneyard.

A voice spoke from above him.

"Command the bones."

Jack turned. He stood alone.

"Call life," the voice said.

A soft breeze lifted Jack's scarf; he raised his hand and plied the material.

"Bones, grow together," Jack said softly.

Nothing seemed to happen.

"Bones, grow together," Jack repeated.

The weeds stirred.

"Bones, grow together."

The air livened like an electric storm.

"Let Kingsbreath raise you."

A mighty wind rushed through the valley. Bones rattled together. They formed into figures. Muscle striations grew across them. New skin spread over them.

Corroded weapons went new.

A figure stood up. No longer a skeleton; the Man was complete. He knelt before Jack.

"Up, brother, we're here to fight," Consistence said.

The entire field was coming alive.

The Man picked up his spotless rifle.

"Good."

*****

Lieutenant Colonel Condemnation jumped from the tank.

"Impressive escape, baby-killer."

Kristian lifted the LOGOS weapon.

The gunshot resounded across the plains, and the Lieutenant Colonel fell to the ground.

Kristian's squad reacted first. The searchers charged their foes: the five hundred fled from twelve.

One searcher grenaded the tanks.

The Janissaires ran towards their fortress.

On the far side of the field, a violent noise arose.

The gray soldiers stopped cold.

Ten thousand healthy, bearded warriors emerged from the haze. They were heavily armed, and Jack Consistence led them.

The searchers who had regained their lives—who had come through ambush, torture, and death—left not a single Janissaire alive.

*****

Kristian's rifle covered the gasping foe.

"You can't win, Searcher."

A smooth voice called out from the haze.

"Kris."

It was the dark-haired woman. She emerged from a forgotten enemy vehicle.

"Don't you want to get to know me?"

She now wore the uniform of his enemies. A patch centered her flak jacket, reading: CAPTAIN LUST.

This time, Kristian had an answer.

"I'm a married man."

The woman laughed with an exaggerated contempt.

"She doesn't love you."

That may be true. But that's not what matters.

"Christi Anders is my high school sweetheart, the mother of my daughter, and the love of my life. Condemnation clouded me for a while, but now I remember the truest thing in my life: that I love her."

Captain Lust dove towards the passenger seat. She tried to reach her rifle. Kristian's weapon cracked, sending tracers through the fuel tank.

At the last instant, Lust flashed to her true form: A frame of black tar with empty eye sockets and terrible alligator teeth.

The white-hot fireball consumed her.

Condemnation sliced his combat knife through the air, but Kristian's heavy boot pinned his arm.

"I will always be here to pull you down," the Lieutenant Colonel spat. Black blood stained his chest.

"If I fall, I will arise," Kristian answered.

"You will never be free."

Kristian slung his rifle. His hand moved to the Snake Slayer in his belt. The hollow point .45 waited for him, chambered and ready.

Kristian considered the years he had lost to Condemnation: his cancered marriage, his stolen daughter, his murdered mentor.

He cocked the pistol.

Fear filled the enemy's black eyes.

Kristian brought to mind the words of the Rifle Manual.

"There is no Condemnation for Prince-finders."

He pulled the slack from the trigger.

*****

Consistence approached.

The grand army stretched behind him.

"Where did you find them?" Kristian asked.

"The Boneyard," Jack said. "The bones grew together. And muscles formed on them. And Kingsbreath lifted them. We loosed the other prisoners, gutted the armory, and burned the stronghold to the ground."

Across the field, the distant fort smoldered in black ruins.

"What about Past?" Kristian wondered.

"He's ashes."

Kristian looked down to his feet, where Condemnation's lifeless body lay.

"Then we're free."

16. TRANSLATED

Jack stood on the edge of the vast water. His hands moved up and down on his scarf.

"This is it." Yearning and hope and promises filled his words.

Kristian followed Jack's gaze. The path and its markers stopped at the water.

"It ends in the sea?"

Consistence pointed to a white stone just beneath the surface. Beyond it, the markers continued into the deeper water.

Behind Jack and Kristian, ten thousand searchers warmed themselves around bonfires.

"As long as there's a path, I'm going to follow it," Jack said.

He shed his combat load.

Kristian looked at the watercolor sunset on the mountains. He turned to the sea.

This could be my end.

But the unknown is only feared by those without the King.

He kicked his boots off.

Kristian's toes sank into the cool mud.

He pulled the book from his pocket. Introduced by John Dabble, summarized by Evan, practiced by Ian, and explained by Pastor. Kristian held it to his chest.

He walked out.

When the water reached his ribs, ominous clouds rolled across the sky.

The sea lifted as hills.

Feet off stable ground, Kristian struck forward.

The rain whipped down, and the waves grew high. Walls of wind flogged the water into a chaos.

But Kristian stayed fixed on the horizon.

The waves hammered and rolled him underwater. When he broke the surface, he saw the water form into cliffs above him.

Every breaker hit upon him, every crash sapped his strength.

A wall of water raised in front of the sky, its galactic height defying imagination.

Kristian's arms gave out. He floated.

This is where it ends.

His eyes came to rest on the shifting lights and dark water below him.

Despite the approach of the thunderous waters, Kristian felt peace.

He smiled in calm confidence.

"I'm ready."

17. PROMOTED

Kristian's eyes flickered open. A soft surface supported him.

He scanned the green field. Red soil held him like a mattress.

His lungs pulled in the freshest, most delicious scents of flowers and stinger-less bees. He could taste the daylight.

Something moved behind Kristian.

Jack Consistence wandered nearby. He didn't notice Kristian. Jack was too busy taking in every sight, every breath of wind, every color on the air.

"I knew it," Jack said.

A man reached down to Kristian. The face familiarized.

"Evan!"

Kristian leapt up to embrace his friend, then he suddenly remembered how they had parted ways.

"The last time I saw you…"

Here Evan stood, clean, refreshed, and youthful, like a warrior on his way to a wedding.

"How are you alive?"

"Kristian, haven't you guessed?"

"That final wave was the end?"

"The beginning," Evan grinned. "Come with me. He's here."

Kristian looked to Consistence. Jack was enraptured with the land, as though every dandelion puff, every dragonfly wing, was the confirmation of words he had studied and trusted, sight unseen.

"Consistence will be along soon."

"What about the others on the far shore, Evan?"

"They will cross when it is their time. Also, my full name here is Evangelist."

Kristian and Evangelist advanced to an overlook.

The colors of this new world shined in their pure forms. It was like the countryside after a rain, when the skies have cleared, and the world is fresh and bright and clean. But here, the washed colors never faded.

The reds and browns of the soil called to Kristian's

soul. For when the universe where Kristian's body originated was formed, so many thousand years ago, formed from a single word, the body of the first man was molded from the soil of that same world. But his mind, will, and emotions were sculpted from this red dirt. The spirit of man, had been breathed from the King's own breath. Though the man's body would ultimately return to its own soil, this older land would always call to the eternal part of him.

Kristian knew it, and his heart rested like returning home.

Tens of thousands of minor waterfalls fed in and out of each other on the left then ran to the spreading sea. On the right, the tallest, most majestic forests spread away forever. Inside their shelter, wonderful animals roamed. In the center of the land, a mountain rose with a view of the entire land.

Evangelist and Kristian strode side-by-side.

They carried no combat load; they kept no equipment of war. They were friends as only men who have conquered war and now taste peace can be. They laughed and talked and visited for the entire journey.

They ascended the chief mountain. The path, dotted with the familiar white stones, ended in an archway of living trees.

The air thickened with a musty heaviness, as though something weighty and ancient and all-important was covered inside the arbor.

Evangelist motioned Kristian to the inner chamber.

"He's expecting you."

Kristian moved through the arbor alone. From the middle of the courtyard, a voice spoke.

"Kristian."

In that moment, Kristian knew he would be called Searcher no longer, for he who has found requires a new name.

"My Beloved," the Voice called.

It was the same Voice who had revived Kristian Beloved in the hopeless dungeon.

Kristian beheld the speaker. The King's wonderful eyes carried a poetry of forgiveness. Acceptance. The corners were upturned in an ever-bubbling joy. He was a true Warrior, more Kingly and Good than anyone Kristian had ever met.

"Am I worthy to be here?" Kristian asked.

"You have been *made* worthy. Now," the King lifted Kristian's face, "Say what you came to ask me."

Kristian remembered his wife and everything he and she had undergone. But now it was as though he remembered someone else's memories, as though all the bitter emotion had been removed from them.

"Can you restore my Wildflower to what she was?"

"Nothing can ever be what it was before."

The King paused, his eyes burning with Joy and

Goodness.

"But I can make it better."

The End.

EPILOGUE PART 1

One year ago.

The man coughed against the heavy blanket of dust.

Kasey peered towards the cloud that Evan had just run through.

Good. He's safe, Kasey thought.

The sound of steel grating on stone pulled his eyes up front.

A grenade.

Kasey knew he couldn't return it in time. His mind counted down:

Three to five seconds 'til it blows.

His vision became super-honed as he scanned for an escape route.

Two seconds left.

He snapped a fresh magazine into his rifle.

One second.

His eyes landed on a fissure in the rock at boot level.

He wriggled inside, and fell several feet onto a hard rock floor. The grenade detonated.

The enemies scanned the area. They soon decided that both men must have escaped through the canyon.

Kasey's eyes searched the cave.

How do I always end up underground?

He took up his rifle with determination, wondering what became of Evan, what became of their mission.

EPILOGUE PART 2

The wheelchair sat empty. Christi hadn't left her bed in months. She hadn't even gotten up when they'd celebrated Sage's sixteenth birthday.

Katy Influence's words babbled with no end. Today's topic centered on Kristian and what an awful husband he had been.

Does she think I need a reminder?

Christi tried to tune her sister's voice out.

He was a terrible husband.

The thought made Christi feel superior in a warped way.

He was unbearable the last few weeks. I bet he was tired of taking care of me. That's why he left.

Christi's eyes landed on the wheelchair. She hated it.

He abandoned me to that thing.

A photo on the wall framed Katy and the two boys. It made Christi sick.

I don't resent the boys...

But it was untrue. Christi hated everything.

Katy talked herself out then she left for the barn.

Alone at last, Christi's eyes clouded. But she stopped the tears from forming.

Her thin hand moved to her wheelchair, where she had stashed the black and white picture.

Her fingers separated the vinyl layers, and she pulled out the image.

She smoothed away the wrinkles.

A sonogram.

Her baby.

If Kris's King were real, if He were good, He wouldn't have let Kris kill her.

She looked to heaven.

"You took everything from me," she said.

Upon hearing herself say the words, her thoughts crystallized. The past decade melted into a single realization: Christi didn't blame Kris for everything.

"I blame the King."

She caught herself.

But how could someone in a faraway land have anything to do with us? Kris didn't even know about Him back then.

Did he?

As Christi held her eyes on the ceiling, hot tears fell onto the dingy bedsheets.

Why would you let this happen? You're not good.

As the thoughts bent Christi's mind, she suddenly wondered why she held such anger towards someone she had never met.

Who are you? I only know what Kris heard from the Wanderer.

I don't know if you even exist.

But in an aching corner of her basement heart, Christi begged that He did.

The Searcher Series will return.

To receive notification for future projects, send an email to wisanpeter@gmail.com.

PETER WISAN

NOTES

ABOUT THE AUTHOR

Peter Wisan is a language collector, adventurer,
screenwriter, and film director. He is a Captain in the
United States Marine Corps Individual Ready Reserve.
His greatest literary influences are
C.S. Lewis, Ray Bradbury, and O. Henry.